O9-CFT-656

Unraveled Stalkings

K.D. McCrite

Annie's®
AnniesFiction.com

Unraveled Stalkings
Copyright © 2014 Annie's.

All rights reserved. No part of this publication may be reproduced, stored in a retrieval system, or transmitted in any form or by any means—electronic, mechanical, photocopying, recording or otherwise—without the prior written permission of the publisher. The only exception is brief quotations in printed reviews. For information address Annie's, 306 East Parr Road, Berne, Indiana 46711-1138.

The characters and events in this book are fictional, and any resemblance to actual persons or events is coincidental.

Library of Congress-in-Publication Data
Unraveled Stalkings / by K.D. McCrite
p. cm.
I. Title
2014908880

AnniesFiction.com
800-282-6643
Annie's Mysteries Unraveled
Series Creators: Janice and Ken Tate
Series Editors: Shari Lohner, Janice and Ken Tate
Cover Illustrator: Kelley McMorris

10 11 12 13 14 | Printed in China | 9 8 7 6 5 4 3 2 1

One

Maybe she'd had too much caffeine late in the day. Maybe she should have watched the Hallmark movie instead of the one on the science fiction channel. Maybe she was hungry. Whatever the reason, Kate Stevens was still lying wide awake at two o'clock on that Tuesday in mid-October. Her mind churned like floodwaters.

She plumped her pillow, smoothed the covers around her, and refused to look at the bedside clock again. Behind closed lids, she could see the mental list she had ticked off a hundred times already, and each item seemed to have equal priority to the one above it. Even now, six weeks after her move from Maine to Texas, anxiety lingered. Worrywart that she was, Kate always felt she had left something undone, somewhere.

"Oh, I give up!" she said aloud and threw back the covers. If she couldn't sleep, she might as well get up. Instead of putting on her robe and slippers, she padded to the dresser, removed fresh underwear, a T-shirt, and a pair of jeans. She took a quick, warm shower and got dressed.

The distinct leftover smell of the fish she had baked for dinner lingered in the kitchen. Although it had enticed her appetite last evening, the odor was now nauseatingly musky. She opened the window above the sink.

A strange sound wafted in with the dry breeze. *Thunk, scrape,* pause. *Thunk, scrape,* pause. The noise seemed to come from her backyard. Kate squinted into the night and saw nothing. She flipped off the light over the sink, plunging the kitchen into darkness and opening her vision of the shadows outside.

As her eyes adjusted to the night, she spotted someone moving. Not in her backyard but at the empty house next door. She leaned closer to the window, peering hard.

What on earth? Someone is digging? Really?

As if the person had felt Kate's gaze and heard her thoughts, the digging stopped, and the individual turned. Kate darted back from the window. After a while, when the digging sounds failed to start again, she ventured a peep outside. She saw nothing but long shadows cast by the live oak tree in her backyard. She stared, her gaze probing every inch of lawn and the facing wall. Where had the person gone? Was he now prowling around her house, maybe in her backyard, or even at her back door a few feet away?

She rushed to it, tested the lock, then hurried to the front door to make sure it, too, was secure. Kate moved quickly and as silently as possible through the darkened house, going from window to window, checking that each one was locked. She peeked through the blinds. No movement out there.

Making coffee in a kitchen lit only by the glowing dials and numbers of appliances proved tricky. The window had only a ruffled valance, and if she turned on the light, she'd be visible to anyone outside. At the mere thought, the tiny hairs on her arms stood. Carefully, she poured coffee into a cup and carried it to the small bedroom she'd turned into a work space and design studio.

Her mind would not leave the image in the backyard. She told herself that perhaps all she'd seen were strange shadows cast by clouds and moonlight. Maybe the digger had been a stray dog looking for scraps.

Or maybe I imagined it.

Surely that was possible. So much had weighed on her mind lately, and sleep had evaded her as if she were its enemy. Kate doubted she'd slept more than two or three hours a night in the past week. An image borne of sleep deprivation—one that was digging around in her head rather than the yard next door—must be the answer. She checked the curtains and blinds before turning on the desk light and booting up her laptop anyway. She didn't feel like doing any serious work, but she might jot down some notes for her next magazine column, or do a bit of research. She also wanted to see what her daughter had been doing. Since Vanessa had started attending Regency College, one of the best ways Kate could keep up with the young woman's busy life was the social media site Friendlink.

The site not only helped Kate keep in close touch with Vanessa, but it provided a way for Kate to get updates from her friends in Maine. It wasn't as good as having her friends around her or Vanessa in the same house, but it was an acceptable second.

She had just clicked on Vanessa's home page when a chime signaled her and a small box popped up at the bottom of the screen. The thumbnail photograph of a handsome, dark-haired man brought a smile to her lips. She and Nick Scott had connected online a few weeks before Kate had decided to move to Texas. Their connection had been a mutual interest in vintage cars.

Actually, Kate's interest had been little more than simple curiosity, seeing if she could create a crochet pattern based on auto designs of the 1930s. A casual remark she had made on the Yesterday's Rides website forum had sparked a response from Nick, and they had traded a few questions and answers about vintage cars. Soon he'd found her on Friendlink, and the two began chatting for several minutes each day. Their communication was fun and superficial, a sharing of ideas and observations, and Kate felt an easy kinship with Nick. Maybe it was because they could chat online without the awkwardness of face-to-face contact.

Her innate shyness was something Kate had vowed to overcome in her life-changing move to Texas, but it often left her feeling ill at ease and at a loss for words.

How odd that he's online at this time of night, she thought as she clicked on the box to read his message.

"Hey, young lady," he had written.

"Hey yourself," she typed back. *"Imagine running into you here."*

"LOL. Come here often?"

"I usually write my column at night, but never this late. Right now, I'm only here because I need to distract myself from spooky goings-on at the empty house next door."

"Don't like the sound of that. What's going on?"

She hesitated. The digging figure may or may not have been real, but the image lingered, and she knew it probably would until she could fully release it from her mind like a bad dream.

"I thought I saw someone digging in the backyard next door." It seemed as though some of her fear lifted a little in the mere sharing of what she'd witnessed.

"When?"

"Just a few minutes ago."

"Is he still out there?"

"No. At least I can't see him."

"Lock your doors and windows!!"

She smiled and hastened to assure him. *"I always do."*

"Check them."

"I just did. Everything is locked."

"DO IT AGAIN! NOW!!"

She sat back in her chair, staring at the screen. She wasn't very proficient in online techniques and texting protocol, but she was pretty sure all caps and multiple exclamation points in text messages meant the person was yelling, virtually. If Nick had been in the room with her right then, he would have been shouting at her. His reaction both irritated and comforted her. She could take care of herself and didn't need anyone pushing her to do so, but it was nice that someone cared enough to push. At any rate, to calm his anxiety, she typed, *"OK, BRB."*

The BRB—"Be right back"—was a bit of texting vocabulary from her daughter that came in handy. Vanessa and her friends were proficient in the shortened language, but Kate wasn't sure she could ever stoop to typing "RU" for "are you" or "TTYL" for "talk to you later."

To appease the anxious Nick, Kate went through her small house again, checking the locks on both front and back doors. She eyed every curtain, every blind, and pressed every window lock. She scoured the outdoors with intense scrutiny once more. At last, knowing she was as secure as she could be in her home, she returned to her office.

"All done. Locks turned good and tight, curtains pulled snug, shades firmly closed."

"Good girl. Now, call the cops."

She blinked, then frowned. That "good girl" remark didn't sit well.

"There's no reason to do that," she typed.

A long pause, then, *"Call the cops."*

Her frown deepened. *"I don't want to bother the police just because I saw shadows. But if I spot anyone prowling, I will."*

No reply showed up for so long that she wondered if her message had gone through or if Nick had just terminated the connection. Finally she closed the chat box and moved on to Vanessa's updates, smiling at the photos and an account of a dinner that she and three of her new college friends had shared the night before. She was just typing a comment into the thread of the conversation when the chat box popped up with a message from Nick.

"I don't know why you won't help yourself," Nick said.

Kate chewed her lower lip and parsed his words. Nick was reading far too much into this. She tried to allay his overworked notions.

"Honestly, I haven't been sleeping well for so long, I probably saw nothing. There is no reason to worry."

"But I do worry, Kate. You worry me. All alone in a strange city, with no one or nothing to trust but yourself and your wits. A beautiful, gullible woman like you is the perfect target for a maniac looking for a victim."

She squirmed, not liking the uncomfortable turn in the conversation. She preferred their chats to remain lighthearted and friendly. Her interactions with Nick had been one way she could escape the concerns of moving to a new place and the annoyances of everyday life.

"I appreciate your concern, but as I said, I've had so much on my mind that I'm sleep deprived. And, BTW, I'm not gullible." She pushed the Enter button, confident her words would calm his concern.

Again she waited longer than his replies usually took, then his response showed up. *"So you'd rather dismiss the entire situation as a flight of imagination?"*

"Yes!" She was so relieved that he understood.

"And you don't mind if someone comes into your home, steals your property, or hurts you? Any rational woman would have already called the cops."

His words seemed written in anger, and that caught her off guard. She reread his comment, then scrolled back and read their entire conversation once more. The easy banter she had shared with him up to this point was a big reason she enjoyed their chats.

Kate wasn't sure how to respond. Maybe she read more into his words than he intended. On the other hand, she felt insulted, as if he were belittling her. Her ex-husband used to do that, making disparaging remarks about her talent, her intellect, sometimes even her appearance. Nick had never been insulting before, not even a little bit.

Maybe I'm too sensitive.

But maybe not. In either case, she refused to feel bad because someone else questioned her decisions or opinions.

"Thanks for your concern, Nick, but I'm fine. I must go now; I have work to do."

She clicked the Send button, then logged out of Friendlink. The exchange left her feeling uneasy and disheartened.

Two

The bell on the door of the Once Upon a Yarn needlecraft shop jangled as Kate stepped into the haven later that morning. If there was one thing that calmed her, it was immersing herself in all things crochet. She loved being surrounded by notions that were the promise of beautiful objects yet to be created. She really missed that about her life in Stony Point, Maine. Working at A Stitch in Time yarn shop, she had been able to spend hours in the company of yarn, thread, notions, patterns, and the people who enjoyed wielding crochet hooks, knitting needles, or quilting hoops.

That morning, she planned to search Once Upon a Yarn until she found the exact yarn she wanted for an evening wrap, something warm enough for a cool Texas night, but not thick and snug like she would have designed for a winter in Maine. She would make the wrap simple and practical, but elegant. The yarn she chose would be the crowning jewel of this garment. She hoped Paige Bryant, the storeowner, had the right yarn in stock.

The shop sat at the end of a strip mall in Fort Worth. Given its location, Once Upon a Yarn could have been boring and generic, but Paige knew how to create a shop that gave customers a charming experience. Muted colors, shining stone floors and small lights lining the ceiling welcomed anyone who stepped inside. Near the door was a small white table with a coffeemaker and china cups, a sugar bowl, and a creamer dispenser. In the corner sat an electric fireplace with four comfortable-looking chairs and a small coffee table cozily arranged for conversation. Faintly, the strains of classical music slipped through the air, just enough to caress the ears of shoppers.

"Good morning!" Paige sang out. Her spunk and vitality belied her years. In her early fifties, she kept her blond hair chin length, fashionably sleek and simple, but her eclectic style of dress was every bit her own. Her effusive personality embraced Kate's shy soul. She was rearranging red shades of yarn in a center cubby display. "You're here early today."

"Hi, Paige. I'm the early bird after that proverbial worm, I guess." She laughed and glanced at the clock above the display of alpaca wool yarn. The store had been open less than fifteen minutes.

Paige dipped her head toward the coffee. "Help yourself to the caffeine. I also have some new tea—red clover and cinnamon. Tastes great, but without the kick you get from coffee."

"Thanks, but I want to look at the yarn. I need something special."

"Special is my specialty." Paige gave her a bright smile as she put down the final skein of scarlet yarn. "May I help you?"

A rush of warm morning air swept into the shop as someone entered.

"I'll let you know if I need you," Kate said, "but I think I remember seeing just what I want when I was in here the other day."

Paige tipped her head to one side. "Do I sense a new design in that brain of yours?"

"You do."

"Ah, a designing woman," said a voice behind Kate. She turned and watched an older man approach. In the morning sun that poured through the front windows, Adam Vargas's thick white hair seemed to give off its own light. His dark brown eyes gleamed with life.

Kate had met Adam at a dinner party hosted by Paige and her husband, Patrick. Within two minutes, Kate and Adam had established a rapport, and by the end of the evening, she felt as though she had connected with an old friend.

"Why, Adam! Hello." She extended her right hand.

Kate had learned that although he had traveled extensively and lived all over the United States, Adam was every inch the Southern gentleman. He took her proffered hand and bowed slightly from the waist.

"So good to see you again, Kate. Good morning, Paige."

"Hello, Adam. What brings you to my shop so early? Are you out catching worms too?"

He laughed. "I need some more of that variegated sea-and-sand yarn. But first," he said, sharing a smile with both women, "I could do with some coffee. Thank you, Paige, for providing refreshments."

"It's my pleasure," she said. "Help yourself. I'd love to offer pastries, but I don't think sticky fingers and yarn should go together."

They laughed, then the phone rang and Paige went to answer it. Adam led the way to the coffee station where he filled cups for Kate and himself.

"Let's sit down for a couple of minutes," he suggested. They walked to the small sitting area and settled down, facing each other.

"How's the literary agent business today?" Kate said after she took a small sip of coffee. "Have you discovered any great talents since I saw you last—perhaps someone who is writing the next Great American Novel?"

He chuckled. "I wish." He opened a yellow packet of sweetener and paused, looking at it, smiling. "I really should give up sweets altogether, or so my doctor says." He met Kate's eyes. "He tells me this stuff will make me crave sugar even more." He opened the packet and stirred it into his coffee.

"And does it?" she asked.

He shrugged and tapped his spoon against the side of the cup. "I don't know, but I know I crave morning coffee." He took what appeared to be a satisfying sip.

"So do I," Kate replied, laughing. "Especially these days." She took a drink.

"It sounds like you need some extra energy."

"And how! I just can't seem to relax."

Adam set his cup down. "Why's that?"

"I think that business a few weeks ago with Betrugen has kept me on edge." She shuddered, remembering how she and her new friend Vivi Lawrence had chased bad guys all over Sage Hills and Fort Worth. Vivi lived across the street from Kate, and the friendship between the two women had grown stronger every day. "Plus, I'm still getting settled. That takes a while, you know. It's been a little tricky, adjusting to Texas life."

"I understand."

"Paige asked me to display some of my designs here for her to sell, so I need to get them made. Soon. I'd like to get my next column written for *Hook and Needle Arts* magazine. Also, I want to put together another book—even though I haven't sold the first one yet. Then there is my yard. It's so plain, and I'd really like to put in some flower beds, maybe even plant a tree or two. And I need to find employment sooner or later." She spread her hands. "It just seems there is so much to do, and all of it needs my attention right now. I don't know where to start!"

"I understand. In fact, I've been where you are, facing new challenges, trying to keep up with life as I've known it, wanting to do it all and feeling as though it's impossible. And it doesn't help that you moved down here because Stefan Betrugen promised you a career with his publishing company. I had a client there, you know, so all three of us got burned by that crooked character."

Kate felt herself melt a little, knowing this kind man traveled the path with her.

"What should I do?" she asked. "Where should I start?"

"Lots of coffee." He lifted his cup, laughing. "Actually, I had to learn to be organized. By nature, I'm a bit of a putterer and shuffler, but if you're self-employed, you can't allow that easygoing nature to take over. So I created a plan for myself, with goals and steps I'd need to take to reach them."

"And you stuck with it. I mean, look where you are now."

"It took me a while. I had to rearrange priorities, weed out what didn't work, devise new plans. Even today I make changes. It's important to be flexible."

Kate sipped her coffee and thought about a conversation she'd had with Vanessa not that long ago. "Being inflexible will make you set in your ways," her daughter had told her.

"I don't want to become stagnant or rigid," Kate said to Adam.

"Right."

She mulled Adam's words over, remembering he had told her that he'd been a successful magazine writer for most of his life. It wasn't until his wife became extremely ill that he had semiretired from that line of work to care for her. After her death, he donned the cloak of literary agent, starting a new career at an age when most men spent their days fishing or on the golf course.

Kate wished she could crawl into his brain and mine the wealth of information stored there. "I just don't know where to start," she said. "Would you help me?" She blurted the question before she had the chance to talk herself out of asking.

He stopped in mid-sip, his eyes steady on hers.

"What I mean is, I think I need an agent," she rushed on. "There is so much I don't know about moving forward with this career. That is, I have a million ideas and know how to sketch them and draft patterns. I can crochet just about anything you can think of, but there is so much more to it than that. Having my designs published would be a big step essential for a career in crochet design. You know the business and financial end of publishing, the contracts, and rights, and copyrights, and ... and ..." She closed her eyes and rubbed her temple. "I'm just so overwhelmed by it all."

"Of course you are," he said quietly. "Your mind is full of ideas. All this dull business puts a damper on it, doesn't it?"

She nodded.

"You need to spend your time creating your designs, not deciphering contracts and small print."

"Exactly!" She opened her eyes, dropped her hand, and beamed at him.

"My agency isn't a big one," he said, as if warning her.

"I know. I'd probably get lost in a big agency."

He chuckled. "Not lost, but perhaps you'd get less attention than you'd receive from a smaller one."

"So what do you think? I'd work really hard, and I'd listen to your advice, and—"

"I would love to represent your work, Kate. In fact, if you had not asked me, I was going to request the honor of being your agent."

"You were?" Her face grew warm. "Thank you so much, Adam! I will do my best to be a good client."

"You'll be a great client. I recognize your talent and I see your passion. I've read all your columns and know you have a gift for simple expression of ideas." He smiled. "Be assured: I'll work hard on your behalf."

They shook hands and grinned at each other.

"When I get back to my office," Adam said, "I'll draw up a contract. In the meantime, here is what I'd like for you to do."

Kate took a pen and pad from her purse, poised her pen above the notebook and nodded.

"Create a Friendlink account," he said.

"Oh, I have one. Vanessa insisted on it. Of course, I've enjoyed it. Lots of fun things to read." She chose not to mention the recent episode with Nick. Her personal concerns were nothing he needed to know.

"I mean a business account. Also, set up accounts with PinMyLife and Chatter." He named several more online social media sites. She scribbled down each one, feeling a mixture of anxiety and anticipation. "Start a blog, and post new updates every week. Write about your enthusiasm for crochet, tell about your experiences, and share a pattern from time to time. You are already admired in the field. Oh now, don't blush. It's the truth. Your columns in *Hook and Needle Arts* have garnered you much praise. Crafters who enjoy being online have already looked you up on the Internet. We must give them something to read and enjoy!"

"I won't have to post a lot of personal information, will I?"

"No!" He shook his head. "Absolutely not. Give your fans enough to know you're real and to connect with you, but be discreet."

"Good!"

"I can send you a contract via email." He snapped his fingers. "Or better yet, let's meet for lunch tomorrow, and I'll bring it with me. Bring me a hard copy of your manuscript."

"I can do that, but I thought you'd want it in an electronic format."

"I do, of course. But let's be realistic. Computers crash. Backed-up files can disappear. The virtual depositories are fine, I suppose, but—well, I like having a hard copy of everything. It's a good practice."

After Adam left, she found and purchased the thread she wanted for the lightweight wrap. The metallic shimmer gave it the aura of moonlit waters.

"I'm so excited for you," Paige said with a huge smile as she put Kate's purchases in a bag. "Just think. A celebrity shops in my store!"

"I'm not a celebrity."

She laughed and handed her the bag. "You will be."

Kate drove home in a daze. *A celebrity? Me? Oh my. What have I got myself into?*

Three

About noon the next day, Kate joyfully signed with the Vargas Literary Agency. Before she and Adam parted company, he handed her some additional pages and reminded her, "Start getting your online presence set up. Publishers like that. This is a good list of tips. I'll email it to you also, but as I said yesterday, I like having hard copies of everything."

"And don't neglect your craft," she muttered as she drove back to her house. She really, *really* wanted to sketch out the pattern for a summery asymmetrical top while the idea was fresh in her mind, make a few items to sell in Paige's shop, and work on the winter wrap.

"There need to be two or three of me!"

A couple of hours later, Kate had set up all the social media accounts Adam had recommended and had created a simple blog site. She stared at the blank page with considerable dismay. *How can a blank screen look so intimidating?*

Gathering the skill she used when writing her columns for the *Hook and Needle Arts* magazine, she began typing about her first experience in crochet. In a couple of minutes, the words seemed to pour from her. When she finished, it was about five o'clock. She sat back and let out a deep breath. Without revealing too much of her private life, Kate had taken her readers on a trip through her development as a crocheter, from first stitch to signing with the literary agency. She referred to the fiasco with Betrugen House as a "blip in the road" and gave no details or names.

Was the blog good or not? Was it what Adam had in mind? At least she'd written something. Deciding to get some feedback before publishing it for the world to see, Kate copied and pasted all three pages to the body of an email and sent it to Vanessa, with a note: "Honey, please give me your opinion of this." She also sent it to Adam, asking for his thoughts and adding, "I've never blogged before, you know!"

She sat back, feeling twitchy and pensive at the same time. After a few moments, she logged into Friendlink. Maybe Vanessa would be online, and it would be nice just to say hi. No sooner had she logged in, though, than a direct message box popped up.

"Hi, lovely lady!"

She blinked. It was almost as if Nick had been waiting for her.

"Hi, Nick." She hit the Send button, not really wanting to chat at that moment, but not wanting to be rude, either. *I hope he's not still in his bossy mood,* she thought. But his next words had the same warm friendliness she was accustomed to.

"Are you having a good day?"

"I am." She smiled about her good news and quickly typed, *"I signed with an agency today."*

"Congrats!"

"Thank you. Launching a new career is scary, but I believe it will be fun once I get the hang of it." She eyed the last bit and added, "I'll be treading further into the world of the Internet than I've gone before. And I've written my first blog."

"Sounds like you've jumped in with both feet."

"LOL. I guess so."

"Be sure to send me links to everything when you get it set up," he wrote.

"For crochet patterns and design??" She tapped the smiley-face icon and pressed the Send button.

"Sure. All of it. And speaking of sending, I want to send you some kind of congratulatory gift. What's your address?"

A tiny alarm sounded in her brain. Yes, she and Nick had been online friends for a while, but she did not know him. She did not even know where he lived, and she had never shared more of her location beyond naming the state.

"It's nice of you to offer, Nick, but unnecessary."

"I want to."

"Really, I don't need a thing."

"C'mon, Katie," he wheedled. "I know better than that. You're a woman. Women always need something. A new dress, a necklace, a box of candy ...."

Kate bristled. For one thing, she did not want to begin some kind of gift exchange with him, and for another, not only did his insistence make her uncomfortable, but his remark was definitely sexist. She tried to think of a polite but firm response, something that would put an end to this thread of thought. Before she could reply, another message popped into the tiny box.

"I know. Flowers! What is your favorite? I'll wire you a bouquet. Or would you rather have a plant, something I can give you that will last?"

The insistent questions annoyed her. Or was she reading more into this than she should?

"That's nice of you, but no thanks."

"Then I'll send you a card. Everyone likes to get a card from a friend, right?"

She hesitated, then typed, *"Thank you for the thought, Nick, but I don't share my address with anyone online."*

A short pause, then his reply almost hissed across the

connection. *"I'm not just anyone. I'm your friend. One of your best friends, and you know it, Kate."*

Did his words carry a hint of hostility? Yes, she thought they did. These last couple of conversations she'd had with Nick had raised red flags. Add the fact that it seemed he had been lurking online, waiting for her, and her concern grew. She needed to step away and think about this relationship. Nick might not be the nice fellow she'd first imagined.

"I need to go now," she typed.

"Don't go."

"I have to get to work."

"No, you don't."

"I do. Goodbye, Nick."

"DON'T YOU DARE LEAVE!!" His anger seemed to roil through the screen.

She closed the message box and turned off Friendlink, as if shoving him away. What was wrong with him? She wracked her brain, trying to recall if at any other time during their online friendship he had sounded threatening or angry. After a couple of minutes, she went back to Friendlink and immediately hid her name from the message box so he wouldn't see that she was online. She opened their archived conversations and sought any hint of a volatile personality. Although she spotted nothing to indicate a short temper, she did note that some of his comments might have meant more than she'd realized at the time.

"Talking to you makes my day."

"I think of you often."

"A beautiful, intelligent woman like you can have anything she wants." This last was said in the context of pondering her move from Maine to Texas. At the time, the words had seemed more supportive than anything else. In fact, when Kate had

read that statement, tears had stung her eyes because she'd so doubted her ability to adjust to a new life.

Was I too open, talking about starting over? Maybe I led him to believe that what he had to say mattered more than it did. Maybe I thought his words meant more than they should have. And if I felt that way, oh, my goodness ... What have I done?

She scrolled back through that particular conversation, looking more closely at each of Nick's responses. Maybe she shouldn't have allowed her fear and doubt to shine through so brightly.

She got up and paced the room. The knot in her stomach tightened. Maybe some fresh air would help.

Outside, she stood for a moment as her gaze wandered next door. The white house with red shutters looked more raggedy than ever. *As if it needs a good dusting,* she thought. Even the windows looked dim in the sunlight.

The lengthening afternoon shadows conjured the memory of someone in the backyard the previous night. She strolled toward the backyard of the other house. Weeds battled grass for growing space on the arid lawn, crowding the area around the foundation.

She examined the area, looking for the freshly dug place. She spotted a few runs made by moles or gophers or some other underground varmints and saw several areas where dirt had been disturbed. Some of it looked scraped and smoothed, while other places looked like they had been drilled. All in all, the yard was rugged and ragged. If someone had been digging, she didn't know where.

She was walking back toward her own house when she glanced across the street and spotted Vivi Lawrence, who was working with a huge potted yellow mum near her front stoop.

"Hey, Vivi," she called.

Vivi looked up and raised a beckoning hand. "Hi, neighbor. Come over and see what I'm attempting to do."

A few years younger than Kate, the blond Vivi embodied the energy and verve of a teenager. Vivi was also a crocheter, and she and Kate had found an immediate kinship from the day Kate arrived in Sage Hills.

"My goodness, what a gorgeous plant that is," Kate said as she reached her friend. She touched one of the flowers with the tips of her fingers. "It's so bright, it's almost like you've captured sunlight." Kate immediately envisioned an embellishment of golden mums on an autumn wrap or jacket.

Vivi smiled and tipped her head to one side as she considered the profusion of blooms.

"Yep. A perfect burst of sunrays. You know me and plants have a rather dismal history, but I understand mums are pretty hardy."

"I think they are."

Vivi glanced around the small yard. "I've been thinking of doing some autumn decorating in my yard this year. Maybe a few pumpkins, a hay bale or two, some gourds. Is it too hokey and traditional?"

"I like traditional at this time of year," Kate said.

Vivi, the quintessential free spirit, beamed. "You know something? So do I, believe it or not. Why don't we do some decorating together on Saturday, your front lawn and mine? It'll be fun!" She practically radiated enthusiasm.

"I like that idea."

Vivi grinned. "You want to go shopping?"

"Right now?"

"Sure!"

For just a moment, a flash of Adam's to-do list burst into her mind and lingered long enough to give her pause, but then she shoved it all aside. Kate liked her neighbor, and she needed to spend time with someone fun and positive. Besides, she had already created the social media accounts. All she needed to do now was become active.

With Vanessa pursuing her own dream nearby at college, and with Paige, Adam, Vivi, and the handsome Fort Worth police detective Peter Matthews as new friends in her life, Kate felt blessed. She shoved aside any lingering thoughts of Nick Scott.

"I need to wash up and change my clothes, then we'll go." Vivi held up grubby fingers and grimaced.

"OK. I'll be ready when you are. See you in a bit."

Kate's glance fell on the house next door to the empty one beside hers. Frieda Mahl, the neighborhood eccentric, was peering through the window, but when Kate raised her hand and waved, the older woman yanked her curtains shut.

"Why did she do that?" she asked Vivi.

"The poor thing is a little daffy. She thinks she's the neighborhood guardian angel."

"Is she dangerous?"

"Not at all. Everyone here takes her in stride. She doesn't bother anyone, so don't worry."

As Kate crossed the street to go back to her house, she felt Frieda's watchful gaze. In spite of Vivi's reassurance, Kate shivered and hurried inside, out of sight.

Four

Kate stretched the muscles in her back an inch at a time and wiped the perspiration off her forehead with her sleeve. It was late Saturday afternoon, and she and Vivi were wrapping up their yard work. "I don't remember sweating like this in October back in Maine."

Vivi laughed. "We'll make a Texan out of you yet. With all the work we've done on our yards today, we're entitled to perspire."

"You should say we're 'glowing.'"

"Yes. *Glowing*. That's us." They giggled together, then stood gazing at their handiwork. Orange pumpkins, golden hay bales, green gourds, and pots of mums of every autumn color filled both yards with cheery, welcoming warmth.

"I think we're finished, don't you? Come inside and have a cup of coffee or tea," Kate said.

"I'd love to, Kate, but I better get to the house. I have a ton of computer work to finish up."

Her reply reminded Kate of the list of tasks she still had to accomplish.

"I have a lot of online work to do too."

"You're among the ranks of today's self-employed women," Vivi said with a broad smile. "No boss standing over your shoulder."

Kate thought of Mary Beth Brock, the owner of A Stitch in Time back in Stony Point. She had never stood over Kate's shoulder. Not only had Mary Beth been her employer, but she'd also been a good friend. Working for her had been a joy and a blessing.

"I realize working for myself comes with a mountain of responsibility," she said, "and there is still so much I need to learn. But I'm determined." She lifted her chin a little higher and arched her stiff back even more. "I'm going to make something of this new life and new career, and I'm going to love it."

Vivi touched Kate's forearm. "Of course you will. I'm still so impressed by your talent and skill. If you stick with it, there is no way you won't succeed."

The words warmed Kate, boosting her confidence. "I admire your ability to juggle so many things at once, Vivi. If I had to plan and oversee all the events at a big hotel the way you do, I think I might fall into a twenty-year faint."

"And if I tried to design so much as a scarf, it would end up looking like an uneven dishrag."

The women shared another laugh. The day had quickly dwindled into evening and stretched long shadows across the neighborhood. Kate couldn't control the uneasy gaze she shifted toward the vacant house next door, and Vivi didn't miss it.

"What's wrong? What are you looking at?" She turned her head and stared at the house, then looked back at Kate. "Kate? What ...?"

Kate gathered her breath and pushed it out slowly. "The other night ..." She paused a moment. "The other night, in the middle of the night, I thought I saw something. Over there."

"Something like what?"

"I'm not sure." She met Vivi's concerned eyes.

"At the Tamblin house?"

"Yes. That place looks worse and worse. You'd think that

since the bank foreclosed on it, they'd try to attract a buyer, but I don't think anyone is doing anything at all. And I'm wondering if it's not attracting vandals or varmints or some other kind of trespasser."

"They've not done a blessed thing," Vivi agreed. She sighed heavily, studying the house. "But what did you see?"

Kate hesitated. "It was probably nothing."

Vivi frowned. "Was someone prowling around?"

"I'm sure it was nothing. An animal, more than likely."

Vivi's face relaxed. "We do have armadillos and possums galore, and they come out at night."

"Then I'm sure that's what it was. We have possums in Maine, but armadillos?" She shook her head. "I've never seen one face-to-face."

Vivi laughed. "Let's hope you never have to. Some people call them 'possums on the half-shell.' They are pesky, smelly things that dig holes in the yard. And they aren't sanitary."

"Eew." What Kate had seen—or thought she had seen—a few nights ago had not been small and four-legged. It had stood on two legs. "We, uh, we don't get bears coming out of the wild here, do we?"

"Listen, Kate, if you see a bear, be sure to call me, the newspaper, and the TV station." Vivi laughed again. "It will be a hot news item." She paused, eyeing Kate again. "Are you all right? Do you want to spend the night at my house?"

She had stayed with Vivi once before. It had been a comfort, and she'd enjoyed it, but she wanted to show grit and strength. "Thanks for the offer, but I'm fine. Besides, I have work to do."

"OK." Vivi gave her a quick, reassuring hug. "If you change your mind, you have my cell number, or you can sprint across the street."

"Thank you so much. I will."

Kate flashed a smile to her new good neighbor. Vivi's presence and friendship had dulled some of the sharp edge of living away from her Maine friends and Vanessa.

I should do something really special for Vivi. I think I'll give her that evening wrap when I finish it.

Kate shot another glance at the empty house next door, but dismissed any more thoughts of the middle-of-the-night digger.

"Listen," Vivi said in parting, "if you get scared this evening, you just call. OK? I know how nerve rattling it can be, being alone, starting over."

"Thanks, Vivi." She held out a hand to her neighbor and they clung briefly to each other's fingers in a gesture of support. "It's good to know you're close."

After her shower, Kate dressed in the camisole and tap pants pajamas she'd bought a few weeks ago and wondered when, or if, she'd need warmer pajamas in Texas. She slipped on a blue-and-white striped cotton robe, fixed a quick supper of a grilled cheese sandwich and soup, then settled down on the love seat with her laptop. She opened her email and saw replies from both Adam and Vanessa.

"Glad UR busy," Vanessa had written. *"U won't have time 2 mope, missing me. LOL. Seriously shorten yr blog post b4 U publish. No one wants 2 read a post that long. Love U."*

Is this the new standard in English? Kate thought. She understood the shortcuts when text messaging, but why in an email?

"At least she answered me," she said aloud. *And offered some advice*, she thought. *But make it shorter? I don't think so. It took too long to write for me to make it shorter.*

She opened Adam's email. *"Kate, you hit the nail right on the head with this blog. It has simplicity, intent, and originality. One problem, though. It's too long. See if you can cut it in half, or less."*

Kate sighed and pulled up the document that contained her blog. She thought what she had written was a perfect blend of bio, dreams, and purpose. If she cut any of it, she would lose its impact. She grimaced.

"Unless," she murmured, leaning closer to the screen, "I do it this way." She highlighted the biography, hit the Cut key, opened a blank document, and pasted it.

That works! Hurray!

She cut and pasted the "Purpose" section and did the same with the "Goals" section.

Three posts from one. Not bad, Kate. She sent the three of them in an email attachment to Adam with a short note asking for his opinion.

At last it was time to do some crocheting—relax her busy, virtual-world-saturated mind for a while. But, like the sirens' song, she felt compelled to check her Friendlink account.

Just for a few minutes to see what my friends are up to, she told herself.

The flag on her chat box indicated twenty-one new messages. All from Nick.

An iron knot twisted in her stomach. She allowed her fingers to hover above the keyboard, pondering the wisest move to make. Should she ignore them? Should she read them and respond? Should she wait and look at them later?

But she knew that if she didn't open the box, the unread messages would torment her. For another moment, she hesitated, then pressed the Open button and expanded the chat box to full screen. She stared, eyes frozen wide, as the messages opened, paragraph after paragraph, filling the screen from top to bottom.

"I hope you've only gone to get a glass of water or cup of coffee," the first message read. He must have sent it shortly after she'd ended their previous conversation.

The next one read, *"Maybe you decided to fix yourself a sandwich. Ham and cheese? Veggie special? You told me you love lots of veggies on your sandwiches. And on your salads. LOL."*

Then, *"OK, I think you've teased me long enough."*

"Are you mad at me? What did I do?"

"Kate."

"Seriously? Kate, are you ignoring me?"

"Why are you jerking me around?"

"I CAN'T BELIEVE YOU HAVE NOT REPLIED!!"

"You better respond to me within the hour. If you don't, you're going to be sorry."

By the time she read that one, Kate was shaking inside herself. How had this happened? A few days ago, Nick was her online friend, full of interest, information, and funny observations.

As her stunned gaze continued down the list of messages he'd left, the screen now started to jump with new ones so fast that the ones she was reading leaped away.

Kate jerked back as though the laptop had caught fire. She pressed her fingertips to her temples as words continued to assault the screen. For a moment, the room seemed to dip and swim. She closed her eyes and gripped the edge of the table until her knuckles ached. She looked at the screen again. The messages continued to pop up. She reached out and turned off Friendlink.

What does this mean? What should I do?

Should she reply, try to reason with him and make him stop? Should she block him? Discharge his friendship? Report him? Call Peter? His law enforcement training had surely dealt with something like this.

She got up and poured a glass of water, then gazed out the kitchen window as she sipped, trying to wash down the huge lump of unease lodged in her chest. *As if a prowler in the backyard next door hadn't been enough to scare me to death, now this, with Nick turning into someone I don't recognize!*

She returned to the love seat and sat down. For a full minute, she gazed at the laptop on the small coffee table in front of her, then turned it on.

She opened Friendlink and ignored the urge to send a final message of explanation to Nick. That would only keep the door open longer than necessary. She found the Discharge Friendship button. She pressed it and cut the friendship.

"There," she said. An unexpected feeling of empowerment shot through her. *Now* that's *how I need to feel more often!*

The doorbell rang, startling her so badly that she nearly fell off the love seat. She sat with her hand on her heart for a few seconds, then moved cautiously to the door. Unease dogged her steps, as though opening it would usher in someone best left uninvited.

Five

Vivi Lawrence stood on the other side of the threshold, the porch light giving her blond pixie-cut hair a faux halo gleam. She carried a tote bag and had a huge smile on her face. The smile fell away the moment she saw Kate's face.

"Kate, what on earth? Are you all right? You are whiter than a bowl of Minute Rice, girl."

The unsettled fluttering in her chest quieted in the presence of her friend. "I'm fine," she choked out.

"You don't *sound* fine." Vivi stared at her through narrowed eyes as she stepped into the house. She closed the door without taking her gaze off Kate. "Did you see something behind the Tamblin house again?"

Kate shook her head and waved one hand toward the love seat.

"Nothing like that," she said. "Have a seat. Would you like some coffee? I can make decaf."

"No, thanks." Vivi perched on the edge of the tiny sofa like a bird of prey. "I don't want to pry—well, yes, actually I do. What's up? Is there anything I can do?"

Someone had told Kate a long time ago that she had an open face. It wasn't until right then that Kate realized the person did not mean her face was broad and wide-eyed; he must have meant her emotions were like headlines streaming across her features.

Her breath whooshed between her lips, and she sank into the chair where she often sat to read or crochet. "Back in July,

I was researching something online and went to a website's forum to ask a question. Long story short, I 'met' a fellow, and we've been chatting regularly since then."

Vivi's eyebrows went up, as if Kate had surprised her. Kate hardly understood why anyone would be surprised.

"Don't you have any online friends?" Kate asked.

"A few. I'd probably have more if I had more leisure time. Anyway, go on with what you were saying."

"His name is Nick. He was friendly and funny. And interesting. In fact, he helped me find the exact design I needed for a men's jacket. On the back it will have the design of a vintage car grill. I promised I'd send him a photo of it when I finished."

"You said he *was* friendly and funny. He's not now?"

"He was. And now he isn't."

"What happened?"

Kate took in a deep breath, pushed it out, and then told Vivi about what had happened with Nick.

"I feel terrible on so many levels," Kate said. "Yes, his change scared me, but I almost feel as if I am going to miss him. Or I should say, I'm going to miss who I *thought* he was. I'll miss our chats and how, during the day, when I'd see something interesting, I'd think, *I'll tell Nick about that.* She met Vivi's eyes. "I was a silly, trusting fool, wasn't I?"

Vivi patted her hand. "No more so than anyone else. All relationships form with blind trust on some level." She hesitated, then asked, "Did you flirt with him?"

"Are you kidding? I don't flirt with anyone." Kate paused. "At least I don't *think* I do. Honestly, I haven't flirted in so long, I'm sure I've forgotten how." She offered a small smile.

"Some people misread our intent," Vivi said. "It's especially true online when there is no eye contact or body language alerting us to intent or deception. It could be this Nick fellow simply took your natural kindness and charm to mean something more than you intended."

Kate wrinkled her nose. "Natural kindness and charm, eh?"

"Maybe that's what happened. You know how guys can be sometimes."

Kate nodded. "I know. I went into the chat history and looked at our conversations. I looked for something—anything—that might have led him to believe I was looking for more than an online friendship. Honestly, Vivi, I didn't find anything like that."

"Would you let me read it? Maybe I can see something that you missed."

"I discharged his friendship status, and doing so deleted all our chats."

"I see. That was the best thing you could have done. Likely he's got the message by now."

"I'm sure." Kate laughed nervously.

"He doesn't know where you live, does he?"

"He knows I moved to Texas, but he doesn't know where."

Vivi winced.

"I know, I know," Kate said. "It just came up when we were talking about the difficulties of relocating. We never really talked about towns—just shared what states we were from. I think he said once that he lives in Michigan. But Wednesday, he just kept asking and asking and asking for my address."

"He never asked for it before now?"

Kate shook her head. "Maybe if he had done so earlier, all this would have come to light and—" She buried her face in her hands. "I just feel so foolish."

"Don't say that, Kate. Making a friend on Friendlink is nothing to be ashamed of. In fact, connecting with and making new friends is pretty much the purpose of social media. You've done nothing millions of others haven't done. "

Kate dropped her hands to her lap and declared, "Well, I'm not using it for that purpose ever again. I have to be online for business, and that's what I'm going to do from now on. No more of this Chatty Cathy stuff. From now on, I'll just call my friends on the phone when I want to know what's going on with them."

Vivi gave a soft laugh. "You don't have to go that far. Just be careful of the friends you choose. Anyway, with all that's on your plate, you're soon going to be far too busy to play online."

"You said it! Adam gave me a list of things, and I've barely scratched the surface." She glanced at the bag Vivi held in her lap. "What do you have there?"

Vivi looked down at her burden and laughed again. "I'd forgotten it! See what a busy brain does for you? It makes you forgetful!"

Kate laughed with her, feeling better by the minute.

"I wanted to bring these over for you, if you want them. These will help you feel more like a bona fide Texan." She pulled out a pair of cowboy boots, intricately stitched brown leather with the obligatory pointed toes and tapered heels. "I bought them for myself, but they are just the tiniest bit too snug at my instep. I think they might fit you."

Kate eyed the footwear, unsure of whether to be pleased or appalled. She'd never given a moment's thought to wearing something so undeniably Western.

"And then there's this," Vivi said. She paused with her hand inside the bag and laughed a little. "I'm almost embarrassed to ask you about this."

"You? Embarrassed? Let me mark this day on the calendar,"

Kate snickered. "You have piqued my interest. What is it?" She leaned forward, trying to peer inside the bag.

Vivi removed a magazine and opened it to a page marked with a sticky note. She tapped a photograph of a cowl-necked tunic. "Do you think this would be too hard for me?"

Kate took the magazine and scanned the instructions.

"I *love* to crochet," Vivi rushed on. "With my crazy schedule, I don't have a lot of time, but I still want to. And I want to make something more than a simple throw or a dishcloth. Isn't this tunic gorgeous?"

"This pattern is rated intermediate. That means it's not extremely difficult, but neither is it an easy pattern."

Vivi gazed longingly at the photo and sighed. "I just want to make it so badly. And in that same vibrant scarlet."

Kate smiled at her friend's exuberance. "Then you will. I'm right across the street, and you can come running to me for help anytime."

Vivi's green eyes shone, and a smile broke out all over her face.

"Would you?"

"Of course! It'll be fun." Kate stood up. "Wait right here." She hurried to her studio, plucked a skein of red yarn, a size G crochet hook, and a thin booklet from the shelves and returned to the living room. She settled down beside Vivi on the love seat. "Here's what we're going to do." She handed the hook and yarn to her friend and opened the booklet. She picked up a pen, checkmarking a few places. "These are the stitches you'll need to know how to do for that tunic. Every day, practice the stitches I've marked. You'll become proficient at making them smooth and even before you know it."

"That would be so great. It'll be fun to have someone as famous as you helping me."

"Famous!" Kate laughed.

"You won first place for original design in that national convention," Vivi said, as if reminding her.

"True. But I'm a long way from being famous. In fact, fame is not something I'd ever chase." She shuddered. "The mere thought of having so many eyes on me nearly gives me hives. If this thing with Nick is any indication, I'd just as soon be anonymous."

"Just be your sweet self," Vivi said, "and you'll be all right, no matter how famous you become."

"I'll make you a deal." Kate lowered her voice and leaned toward her friend as if about to spill a confidence. "I'll help you crochet better than you ever thought you could if you'll help me become a full-fledged Texan."

Vivi beamed and held out her right hand. "Deal!"

After Vivi went home, Kate printed copies of her blog posts and put them in a folder. She closed her laptop and stood for a moment, fingertips lingering on it.

Vivi had said Nick was no longer anyone she had to worry about. Kate hoped she was right. She swallowed back her anxiety and went to bed.

Six

Adam loved Kate's idea of breaking down her initial blog post into three.

"Remember, you need to write something regularly, because you will have subscribers." It was Sunday afternoon, and Kate had invited him to her house for coffee. "Be innovative, prolific, and dependable, and you will build a loyal fan base."

"I'll do my best, but my goodness, I didn't realize I would be spending so much time promoting my business. For some reason, I had visions of doing nothing more than sketching, drafting patterns, and crocheting."

"I want you to publish your first blog post today, then provide links in your status updates on all social media. Publish the second installment in a few days, and the third a few days after that. Keep up with it. And another thing: You will need to get involved in blog tours from time to time. That will help spread your name and reputation."

"Blog tours? What's that?"

"You will be interviewed via email and featured in a variety of blog sites. Think of a television tour without leaving home."

"Oh. Well, I'd rather do a blog tour than be interviewed on television. I don't like everyone looking at me."

"Kate," he said quietly, "your shyness is endearing, but your talent is such that you are going to be garnering a lot of attention in the crafting world. You're going to be asked to speak to groups, teach classes, meet people. I daresay you'll be invited to speak on TV from time to time." She ignored the fluttering in her stomach because she had a feeling Adam was right. She'd just have to become braver than ever, that was all there was to it.

After Adam left, she published her first blog post as he'd recommended, and provided links on all the sites where she had set up accounts. She told herself that technology surely had brought changes to the world. She hoped she could keep up with them because they seemed to change almost daily.

The next morning, she went outside to look at her lawn display, checking to see if the mums needed water. At one point, she glanced up and spotted movement on Frieda Mahl's porch. The woman stepped back, as if hiding, but Kate could still see her. She was thin, dressed in a long dark bathrobe. Her fluffy white hair flowed over her shoulders and down her back, nearly to her waist. But she stood as though made of stone, watching Kate.

Kate lifted one hand in greeting, but the woman remained unmoving. Withering beneath that stare, Kate moved a small pumpkin a few inches to the left and straightened a maverick cornstalk, then went into the house. *Maybe I should have marched down the sidewalk and introduced myself,* she thought. But she had a feeling Frieda wouldn't like that idea any more than she did herself.

For dinner, Kate put a frozen pizza in the oven and poured herself a large glass of apple cider. Then she carried her laptop to the sofa where she turned it on and launched her Internet browser. Without Vanessa at home, meals had become random, eaten only when she was hungry and often consumed in places other than at the dining table. She planned to update her Friendlink status and peruse the updates from her friends while she ate.

As if I'm fifteen years old, she thought, shaking her head and giggling. She most assuredly would *never* tell Vanessa that she had eaten her dinner on the sofa.

She opened Friendlink first and updated her status to "Beautiful autumn day in our town. I'm loving this warm Texas weather." She thought of the coming days and added, "Many new crochet projects are on my horizon. In fact, I have so many new and fun ideas that I'll not run out of work for a long time."

She had a message from Vanessa. *"Hey Mom. Won't c u this wknd. Zoe & I going to Maddie's. Luv u."*

Kate sighed, feeling her daughter leaving the nest more and more. But she was glad Vanessa had friends and a busy life. *Sooner or later, every mother has to let go,* she reminded herself.

There were no more messages in her box. Thank goodness, deleting Nick's friendship had done the trick.

She noted a blue flag icon at the top of the page indicating that someone had requested her friendship. She clicked on it and read, "Beverly Amos requests your friendship."

Her experience with Nick Scott had taught Kate nothing if not to be careful whom she friended online. She clicked the woman's profile. The picture showed a sweetly smiling gray-haired woman who was probably in her early seventies. She held a crochet hook in one hand and a skein of yarn in the other. Her short bio read, "Widowed with no children except my fur babies. Love to crochet and knit. My motto: You can't have too much yarn."

Kate pressed the Accept key. This woman was the kind of person she wanted in her "fan base," as Adam had called it.

Shortly after she accepted the woman's request, a message from her popped up in the chat box: *"Thank you so much for friending me."*

Kate blinked. *My goodness, that was fast.*

"You hooked me with, 'You can't have too much yarn," she typed. *"My sentiments exactly."*

"LOL. I love what you're doing."

Kate paused, unsure what Beverly meant.

"What's that?"

"Your blog! I think it's great."

"Thank you. I published my first post only yesterday. I wasn't sure if anyone had found it yet."

A long pause, then, *"A widow my age has a lot of time on her hands. Since my husband passed, I spend most of my time crocheting."*

Kate's soft heart ached. She understood loneliness.

"I'm sure. It's hard to be alone, isn't it?"

"Yes! Are you widowed too?"

"Divorced. Daughter in college."

"I have no children, just a couple of fur babies. Do you have any fur babies?"

"No pets."

"I have cats. More than I should. Maybe too many, but I do love them."

Kate smiled, remembering Boots, the gray cat back in Stony Point that Annie Dawson had inherited from her grandmother. A beautiful animal, but a bit spoiled.

"Cats are great. Unfortunately, I'm allergic," she wrote.

"That's too bad. Cats can be such easy companions. Maybe someday you can have a dog."

"Maybe. Right now I have plenty to keep me busy, so I don't think I'll get a pet just yet."

"I understand. It's good that you are busy. Kate, it's so lovely to connect with you here on Friendlink. I've been reading your column in the Hook and Needle Arts magazine, and admire your work."

"Why, thank you very much."

As she and Beverly chatted, she felt a warm connection between them. It was nice to have a new friend, a motherly type of person and someone she didn't need to be leery of.

When the timer on the stove buzzed, she typed, *"It's been so nice to chat with you, Beverly, but my pizza is ready."*

"I see. Well, thank you again for accepting my friend request. Not many people my age are online, and I don't seem to have much in common with the young ones. You are the exception."

"LOL. I'm not exactly one of the young ones. Just ask my daughter. I need to go now, but we'll talk later."

"Thank you again."

The thumbs-up icon appeared on Kate's chat screen, then she logged off.

As she ate, Kate again thought about her work and her time, wondering how she would get everything done. Adam had taken on the burden of finding her a publisher, but he had given her tasks that seemed to be even more time-consuming. But if she wanted a career in designing rather than a job as a shop clerk or a waitress, she would have to work to build it. The challenge was daunting, but she knew she could do it.

How was she going to fit time in to create the designs that filled her mind? How would she have time even to crochet them? She felt the quiet throbbing of a fresh headache beginning at the back of her neck.

Echoing suddenly from her past came Harry's voice in

one of his bursts of temper: "Kate, you are little more than a child—a weak-willed woman who will never amount to anything more than someone's underling!"

There were times, especially when he'd been drinking, that Harry had the knack for decimating her confidence. He could make his words seem logical, even truthful. Too long she had accepted those harsh assessments and often stopped herself from expression or action, doubting her abilities. Back in Maine, Mary Beth had helped Kate tremendously with her lack of self-esteem. Now she was able to shake off the memory as the ugly, nasty lie it was. Look how Vivi manages her time. Remember how Mary Beth ran a business and still had a life of her own beyond work? I might not have the business experience that they have, but I'm certainly as smart as they are. And my confidence may be a long way from where it should be, but it's growing stronger every day. For years I took care of Vanessa and myself with little or no help from Harry! A weak-willed woman could not have done that.

Adam had mentioned his action plan. Kate knew if she tapped into the part of herself that was creative and driven, she could build a solid foundation. She could do it.

She opened a blank document on her laptop and began to make her own action plan. By the time she finished, midnight had come and gone, but she felt she had created a good plan, complete with each day's steps to help her reach her goals. Beyond the goals for her crochet work, she had added, "Take care of health," and among the steps she needed to take were getting proper nutrition and getting much more rest.

By 2 a.m., though, she decided getting plenty of rest was going to be a difficult step in her plan. Even a cup of chamomile tea and a warm bath with lavender bath salts didn't help. She crawled into bed, plumped her pillows, then stared up at the darkened ceiling for so long that she wondered if she should get up instead of trying to sleep. Maybe there was a good flick on the classic movie channel.

She grabbed a pillow and a soft crocheted throw, then padded into the living room to settle on the love seat. She had just picked up the remote control when she heard the noise. *Thump, scrape,* pause. *Thump, scrape,* pause.

Kate froze, moving nothing but her eyes as her vision probed the dimness of her unlit living room. The dark, the sound, her unease—all of it echoed what had happened a week ago. This time, though, she knew full well she was wide awake. She was going to find out whatever was creating that unsettling noise.

bed. She [illegible] plumped her pillows, then stared up at the [illegible] that she wondered if she [illegible] trying to sleep. Maybe there was [illegible] channel.

She [illegible] and a soft crocheted throw, then [illegible] the living room to settle on the love seat. She [illegible]

Kate [illegible] as her vision [illegible] the living room [illegible] what had happened a week ago [illegible] well she was wide awake [illegible] whatever was creating that unsettling noise.

Seven

Kate crept off the love seat and stole into the kitchen. She unplugged the microwave and coffee pot, dousing the small amount of light offered by their clocks. Confident the darkness inside her home masked her presence, she peered out the window above the kitchen sink. The wind stirred and the live oak in her backyard shot writhing shadows across the back lawn of the house next door. When her eyes adjusted, Kate discerned deliberate movements.

What she saw was not a small, four-legged creature, nor was it a fearsome bear or wild canine. A thin figure in dark clothes, fully human, chopped at the earth with a hoe or mattock, paused to scrape at the hole, then resumed digging. As she watched, it was almost as if the figure did a dance while digging. He moved from one side to the other after three chops into the dirt.

Whatever he was trying to do next door, he didn't dare do in the daylight. He obviously wanted it hidden.

At one point, while his back was to Kate, he froze. Not a muscle moved, not even a twitch of the hand. Then, with deliberate slowness, as if sensing Kate's gaze, the person began to pivot, not a simple twist of the neck, but a complete body turn. The figure turned completely and seemed to stare right at her. Although Kate knew she could not be seen, her blood ran cold and she felt as though something menacing had skimmed across her body.

She swallowed hard and fought the urge to flee, to hide,

to cower in safety until morning light. Instead, she stood stone still and stared back, taking in every detail she could possibly memorize. Her heart thumped so hard against her chest, she was sure she shook the floor.

Maybe the prowler did more than sense her presence. Maybe he could actually hear her thundering heartbeat.

Her wide-staring eyes burned with dryness. She blinked once, hard, to clear her vision, and when she opened them, the specter was gone.

"Wha ...?" She squeezed her eyes shut once more, clenched her jaw with all the power she possessed, and forced her eyes open again. She saw nothing but the dancing shadows of the trees against the lawn and across the side of the house.

How had the person moved that quickly, that silently? And where had he gone? As had happened before, Kate feared he'd crept to her own house. If he had truly seen her, then he very possibly might try to get to her.

Strength rushed into her body, and she dove toward her cellphone where it lay charging on the countertop. Her fingers shook as she punched in 9-1-1; her voice quivered when she said, "Please send someone to 1911 Hawkins Drive. There's a prowler next door."

A couple of minutes later, with huge relief enveloping her, Kate welcomed the striating lights of the approaching police cruiser. Even so, she nearly jumped out of her skin when her doorbell chimed.

"It's the police," an officer called.

She hurried to the door. "Thank you for getting here so quickly."

The officer was an older fellow with a ruddy complexion and tired eyes. "You reported a prowler?"

She nodded and stepped back to let him enter. "Yes. In

the backyard next door. Actually, I thought I saw someone the other night too." She gave a nervous little smile. "I've not been sleeping well, and I've been under a lot of stress ..." She broke off, realizing she was yammering rather than communicating.

"Anyway, I saw someone over there again just a little bit ago. It's suspicious that anyone would be prowling around an empty house in the middle of the night. Tonight, I think he saw me. I mean, he looked right at me through the kitchen window, even though it was dark in the house, and I was afraid ..." She swallowed back the tears that threatened. "I was afraid he'd come after me because I saw what he was doing."

"What was he doing, ma'am?" He held a pen over the small notebook he took from his pocket.

"Digging. I think. Something like digging."

"Digging? Like a big hole?" He scribbled something, then looked up.

She shook her head. "It didn't look like a big hole. It was just ... *weird*."

"Weird."

The man looked at her as if he thought she was the neighborhood busybody crackpot. She squelched the urge to apologize. If there was some kind of crazed loony-toon in the vicinity, she had every right to report him and be safe. No cop with the look of a well-worn hound should make her feel foolish.

"*Weird*," she repeated. "Don't you think it's strange that someone digs around in the backyard of a vacant house in the middle of the night?"

"Yes ma'am. Can you describe this person?"

"I didn't see him very well, but he was dressed in all black.

Average height, I guess. Height is hard to gauge from this distance and in the dark. There were a lot of shadows, so ...."

He jotted down some words, then said, "You said you haven't been sleeping. You sure you didn't just see some shadows from trees or bushes?"

She sucked in a deep breath and pinned a hard look back on him. "No, I did not. I thought it might be that the first time, but this time I know I saw a person. With a head and arms and legs and feet and hands!"

He crimped his mouth and wrote a few words. He turned his eyes to scour the room, as if he'd find mysterious shadow figures in the corners or under the furniture.

"So did you see where this person went?"

"I didn't. I shut my eyes, just for a second, and he disappeared."

He gave her a dead gaze. "You shut your eyes."

"Like this." She demonstrated the hard blink she'd used earlier. "You know, because I'd been staring so hard."

"And this ... *person* disappeared? Like in a puff of smoke?"

Kate's mouth flew open. "No! And I did *not* imagine any of this! Why would you even think I'd ...?"

She stopped talking, realizing the man was unreachable, and probably unreasonable as well. If she'd been lying in a pool of blood, maybe he'd have been more inclined to believe her.

"We'll take a look around," he said, turning from her. "Lock your doors and windows." He paused at the doorway, giving her a weary once-over. "If I were you, I'd try to get some sleep."

"Thank you for that helpful suggestion," she said, her voice quivering. "I feel ever so much better now."

He touched the brim of his hat as if he believed her and walked away. She shut the door, locked it, and then retreated into the bathroom, where she splashed cold water on her face until her cheeks felt numb.

She gazed at herself in the mirror—at the dark circles beneath her eyes, the paleness of her skin except for the rosiness brought by cold water.

Her doorbell chimed and a voice called, "Kate! Are you all right?"

Kate dashed out of the bathroom to the living room and threw open the front door for Vivi.

"Why are the cops here?" Vivi stood in a floral robe and no shoes.

Kate stepped back and Vivi entered, wide-eyed.

"I'm all right, but I had a scare," Kate said. "I saw someone in the backyard next door again."

"Oh, dear." Vivi clutched the neck of her robe, pulling it snugly. "My goodness. Not an animal then?"

"Definitely a person."

"Did you see who it was this time?"

Kate shook her head. "Not really. Tall, thin—that's all I could tell."

"That's not much to go on." Vivi put her hand on Kate's arm and walked with her to the love seat. "You're shivering. Let me make you some tea."

"That's sweet of you, but I'm OK. Just a little shaken up." She cast a wary glance toward the door. "This is Texas. I might buy myself a big ol' shotgun."

The notion of her purchasing a firearm—and using it—made her laugh in spite of events. Oh, how she'd love to share this story with the Hook and Needle Club and watch the women react. But she wouldn't do that. She was building a new life, and she planned to peel away the dependent layers of her old life. She loved her friends in

Maine, but she was making new friends here, and in time, she'd feel completely at home.

"Vivi, why did you come out with no shoes?" She jumped up and went into the bedroom where she got a pair of mauve slippers she'd crocheted from soft chenille yarn. "Slip these on. Maybe I should make us hot chocolate."

"Thank you," Vivi said, smiling, but still obviously worried. She put the slippers on. "Did he try to break in or anything?"

"I don't think so."

"Did you see where he went? Did he go toward my house?"

She shook her head just as the doorbell rang again. Both women looked at the door warily, but Kate glanced through the peephole and saw the same tired officer.

"No one out here, ma'am, nor around any of the houses nearby," he said when she opened the door. He sighed heavily. "We saw no real signs of digging next door, except where armadillos have dug for insects. You're safe."

"Thank you."

She shut the door, fully realizing the Sage Hill police force thought she was a complete nutcase.

"You care if I spend the night?" Vivi said. "I really don't fancy the thought of going back outside in the dead of night."

A great wash of relief flushed through Kate. "I'd love to have you stay. I was going to crochet and watch an old Doris Day movie. You can join me, if you'd like."

"I'd like to, because I'm wide awake now. But oddly enough, I failed to grab my hook and yarn when I ran out of the house to see what was going on over here."

Kate admired Vivi's ability to make a joke even when a situation was tense. She laughed and said, "That's no problem. I have plenty."

"Then I'm making hot chocolate," Vivi declared.

Kate lent Vivi the materials with which to practice her stitches, and they sat like two schoolgirls, sipping hot chocolate and giggling.

"I have a feeling you might regret this late night when you go to work in a few hours," Kate said.

Vivi waved one hand dismissively.

"As I said, I'm wide awake. Even if I went to bed, I wouldn't get to sleep anytime soon. I'll just make my coffee extra strong when I get there."

They nibbled, sipped, and crocheted as they watched Doris Day try to convince Rock Hudson that he wasn't nearly as sick as he thought he was.

"Crazy how we can talk ourselves into feeling or seeing something that isn't real," Kate said at one point. Had she talked herself into seeing someone next door where nothing had been?

"No!" Vivi said as if reading her thoughts. "You saw something going on, and when the sun comes up, you and I are going to figure out who it was and what they were doing."

Eight

The early morning air was cool with a little breeze. The sun barely peered above the horizon as Kate and Vivi walked into the backyard next door.

"I studied the scene last night from the kitchen window, so I know exactly where that person was," Kate said. She went to the spot, but even though she'd marked the place in her mind, it took her a minute or two to find what she was looking for: fewer weeds than anywhere else in that scrubby yard.

"I don't see any holes other than the ones varmints make," Vivi said, bending and squinting at the earth.

"But I *know* I saw someone gouging into the dirt."

Kate refused to think she was going off the deep end, imagining spooky scenarios, and making what the police probably thought was a nuisance call. Good thing she hadn't called Peter. Her embarrassment would have known no bounds.

She squatted near the rough patches and Vivi hunkered beside her. They ran their hands across the dirt, poking their fingers here and there. There had been no rain in the last few weeks, and the ground was dry and unyielding. Then Kate's index finger sank into a place that was as soft as firmly packed flour.

"Here it is!" she almost shouted. "I didn't imagine it after all."

"The police probably checked this area, but they couldn't see this spot very well in the dark."

"He had a flashlight," Kate said grimly. "I don't think he looked very hard, and that's why he didn't see anything."

"You're probably right."

A moment before, Kate had been glad she hadn't called Peter. But if she found anything in this loosened soil and decided to tell him about her concerns, she could share what had happened and not sound like a kook.

Gingerly but with considerable enthusiasm and nearly overwhelming curiosity, Kate began to scoop away the dirt with her hands. The area wasn't big enough for both of them to dig, so Vivi watched with great interest.

"What do you think we're going to find?" Vivi asked.

Kate's mind buzzed with the possibilities of what lay within the hiding place. "At least it won't be a dead body, not in such a small hole."

"But what if it's a dead animal? A bird, or someone's pet?" Vivi said.

Kate leaned back, grimacing. Did she really want to touch a carcass with her bare hands?

She was just about to get up and fetch a pair of gardening gloves from the house when a strident voice pierced her eardrums.

"Stop that," the voice commanded. "Stop it, I say!"

Kate lifted her head to see someone charging toward them, long white hair flying wildly about her head. It was her neighbor, Frieda Mahl, from two doors down. She felt her eyes go wide, and her heart nearly stopped. She'd never seen her neighbor up close; she looked like a specter from a horror movie.

"What do you think you're doing?" the woman shouted, even though she was now only twenty feet away.

"Frieda—my goodness!" Vivi said, getting to her feet. The older woman ignored her, focusing her glare on Kate.

Kate swallowed and found her voice. "I saw someone over here digging around. I want to know why he was digging.

Did you see anyone?"

"Maybe it's none of your business!" Frieda screeched, her eyes flashing. "Maybe there is a reason someone was here in the middle of the night! Maybe you need to go back home and leave it all alone!"

Shading her eyes against the rising sun with one hand, Kate ran her gaze from grizzled head to grimy bare feet, taking in the woman's build and stance.

"It was *you*, wasn't it? Scrabbling around back here in the dirt?" She didn't bother to keep the accusatory tone out of her voice. "Why were you doing that?"

The woman did not blink, did not back down. She rested her fists against her hips. "What gives *you* the right to pilfer in places that don't belong to you?"

Of all the nerve!

"I could ask you the same thing."

"I take care of our neighborhood," Frieda snapped. "*That's* what I'm doing! I don't know about you. That's always been my responsibility. Ask Vivi. She depends on me, always has. Everyone does."

"This house is empty." Kate pointed to it.

"Yes, it is." Frieda's voice took on an imperious tone. Kate suspected she knew more. Much more. "It has been vacant far too long. But I took care of that." She paused, her glare hardening even more, if such a thing were possible. "If you haven't ruined everything."

"How could I ruin anything? All I tried to do was find out why you were digging in the backyard of a vacant house in the middle of the night."

"Frieda," Vivi said, "tell us what you were doing. Please?"

The woman huffed. "I was bringing buyers," she said as if they should have already known.

"I beg your pardon?"

"I was bringing buyers. More specifically, the right buyer. To this house."

Kate and Vivi exchanged glances, then stared at Frieda, waiting for her to tell them more. Frieda pushed back her wild white tresses and tried to tuck them behind her ears.

"I have a gift," she said. "I use that gift for good. Vivi knows."

"A gift?"

"Of course you do," Vivi soothed. "But what were you doing here last night?"

"I mixed a few things together, along with a poem I wrote. I wrapped them all in muslin, soaked the bundle in buttermilk, and buried it. The charm will bring the right buyer. She glared at Kate. "If you don't mess with it. If you dig up the charm, the interference could bring the wrong buyer. We don't want bad people in our neighborhood!"

Recalling something Vivi had told her a few weeks ago, everything fell into place in Kate's mind. Frieda fancied herself a woman of magical powers. According to Vivi, she often scattered powders or bits of crushed flowers up and down the street.

"We put up with her antics," Vivi had said, "because she's a dear person who spends far too much time alone. But she prefers it that way, and she's completely harmless. Everything she does is concocted to bring about good things."

"Do her charms and spells work?" Kate had asked with a strong touch of humor.

"Of course not! But it pleases her to think she is helping us."

Kate pushed herself into standing position, dusting off her hands and the seat and knees of her jeans. She certainly did not want to make an enemy of any of her neighbors, but apparently she was off to a great start with this one. She decided to try to fix that.

"I'm sorry if I messed with your work," she said in her kindest voice. "I only scooped out a little of the dirt. If you were to put it back, wouldn't your charm still work?"

"Perhaps."

"I think that would work beautifully," Vivi added. "It might even make your charm stronger. Don't you think, Frieda?"

"We can only hope," she said as she dropped to her knees and reverently refilled the hollow Kate had made. With tender hands she patted it, first on one side then on the other, then back and forth. She sat for a moment, eyes closed, hands resting on her thighs. At last she stood. "Let's hope I banished the bad energy before any damage could be done."

Bad energy? Oh, dear. Kate hoped the woman did not pull a doll from her pocket and start pricking it with pins.

She held out her right hand. "I'm Kate Stevens. I live on the other side of this house. Right there." She dipped her head toward her place.

The woman stared at the proffered hand. "I know where you live." Slowly she held out hers. Her palm was as rough as a farmer's calloused paw against Kate's. The handshake was firm, almost painful, but Kate refused to wince, wondering if the woman was testing her.

"I'm Frieda Mahl. I've lived in that house since it was built."

"Then you've been here a long time."

"Frieda has been here longer than anyone else," Vivi said.

"First house in the subdivision," Frieda said proudly.

"Would you like to come over to my place and have some coffee or a cup of tea? You can tell me more about Hawkins Drive and the neighborhood."

"That's a wonderful idea," Vivi put in. "I have to go home and get ready for work, but it would be so nice for you ladies to get acquainted."Frieda's glance bypassed them both to settle on Kate's house. She crimped her lips sideways as though in thought.

"I usually don't go into anyone's house but my own."

"Never?"

"Almost never. I don't like the vibrations."

Kate could come up with no suitable response to that.

"You've been in my house, Frieda," Vivi said.

"Only once or twice." She shifted her gaze to them. "I expect neither of you feel the walls and floors of other houses vibrate, so you don't understand what it's like. In my house, the structure is solid around me. None of this wavering around."

"I see."

"You *don't* see," Frieda said, tipping her head to one side, "but it doesn't matter." She dropped her gaze to the disturbed ground below them. "Make sure you don't touch this spot again. We have to give it a chance to work."

"All right."

The woman lifted her head and shook back her hair, tucking it behind her ears again.

"And never call the cops on me again. In all the years I've lived here, no one has ever called the cops on me."

"How'd you know ...?"

"How did I know it was you that did it? Because no one else would dare."

"Did they come to your house?"

"Of course not. I hung a white thread and a blue thread on the front doorknob."

Kate blinked. "OK," she said slowly.

"You wouldn't understand. You don't believe."

Frieda pivoted and walked back to her house without another word. Kate watched her go, feeling both amused and discomfited. Although she did not believe in magic, spells, charms, or any of that other "woo-woo" stuff, she didn't want to be on the bad side of any neighbor.

"Do you think I've made an enemy of her?" she asked Vivi.

"Oh, I don't think so. You're a nice person. She'll probably come to like you sooner or later."

But it seemed to Kate that if pushed, Frieda might actually cause trouble, with or without magic.

concluded. Ultimately she did not believe in magic spells, charms, or any of that other hocus-pocus stuff; she didn't want to be on the bad side of [illegible].

"Is good luck for me [illegible]," she asked Wyla.

"I don't think so. Wyla's not the person. She'll probably come to like you sooner or later."

But it seemed to Wyla that if [illegible]. Lide didn't actually [illegible] mother with or without magic.

Nine

Early Tuesday morning, after a steaming bowl of oatmeal with raisins and brown sugar, Kate settled down to work. She had printed four copies of her action plan. One was at her desk, another in her leather portfolio where she kept her sketches, another in the bedroom on the bedside table, and the fourth was in a file folder in a drawer.

I have no excuse not to follow this, she told herself as she placed each copy in its designated spot. *I can see it when I wake up, when I sit down to work, take it with me, and I have an extra copy for "just in case."*

According to that action plan, she would read and answer all emails first, make any necessary phone calls, then write for thirty minutes on her blog post. After that, she would check in with social media and update any progress. The afternoons were to be dedicated to design or doing research, and her evenings were to be left free to do as she pleased.

Maybe even go out on a date if I want to, she thought. The image of Peter Matthews leaped into her mind immediately. They hadn't seen each other since the reception for her a few weeks ago hosted by Paige Bryant at Once Upon a Yarn. *I'm sure I'll see him soon.*

At one point, Adam called to ask how everything was going. She felt no pressure from him, but she did sense an underlying concern, as if he sensed the anxieties of last night and the confrontation with Frieda earlier that morning.

"Everything is going well. I've drawn up an action plan."

"Have you? I'm delighted."

"Yes. You inspired me."

"That's what I like to hear. Tell me about it."

She explained in detail all the steps she had created.

"I think that's marvelous, Kate. The best way to get anything done is to work on it doggedly, with purpose. I would suggest, though, that you be flexible enough with your time that you can fit in those conferences and tours we mentioned earlier. I am emailing you a list of websites I want you to peruse. Familiarize yourself with them because later, we hope you'll go on blog tours there."

"OK." She jotted down a note to herself to work in time for this sort of thing. "Adam, thank you so much for all your help. I didn't realize an agent would do so much for a client."

"Many agents only try to sell books to publishers, but I like to help my clients beyond that. That's the advantage of being a smaller agency. So, you're in good hands, my dear. As a matter of fact, the main reason I called was to let you know that Alexus Lauren at Brighton & Craig Publishing is reading your book proposal today."

A tiny spark, like a candle's new flame, leaped inside her. "Really? That was quick!"

"Your magazine publisher knows Alexus and put in a good word for you. In fact, Alexus worked for *Midwest Beat* back when I wrote for them. She's a great editor, and Brighton & Craig is one of the best crafting publishers out there. They have offices all over the world. If they decide to take your book, you'll be in tall cotton."

"Adam," she said, her voice quivering, "I'm all weak-kneed."

He laughed. "How are you going to react when Alexus accepts your submission?"

"I'll faint."

"No you won't. You aren't some Victorian hothouse flower."

She drew in a deep, fortifying breath and blew it out slowly. "I knew we were a good team. I'm so lucky to have you on my side."

"And I, you. Now we both need to get back to work. Lots to do."

"Talk to you later."

She poured a glass of iced tea and then opened the email account she had created solely for her social media accounts. It was something she had not checked since she made it, thinking it was only for verification and notifications from the various social media sites she'd joined.

It dismayed her to find that with the exception of Friendlink, she found notifications from every site with Nick Scott's name on it as a subscriber, a follower, or a buddy. She hoped he would not be so over-the-top with his posts on these sites, but her heart sank with dreadful expectations.

Grimly, she opened her Chatter account first. With only a hundred and forty characters allowed, the posts were short, but there were many of them. A few were related to crochet sites and shopping, but nearly all the rest of them were from Nick.

"I found you!! Let's chatter, my special friend. #bestfriends #hugs #don'tleaveme" was the first one. She stared at the hashtags, completely disheartened. As she scrolled through, reading them in the sequence they had arrived, she found simple updates from him: *"Off to dinner at my fave place. Wish @KateStevens was here!" "@KateStevens. I couldn't sleep last night. Could you?"* On the surface, there was nothing offensive or unsettling about anything he had written. In fact, if she hadn't known better, she would have thought Nick Scott was a young man, sharing updates with his friends.

Maybe that's it, she thought. *Maybe Nick is just a kid. I know his original Friendlink account photo was probably a stock image, so I really don't know what he looks like.*

Nevertheless, she refused to take any chances by offering him the benefit of the doubt. He might be a kid; he might be an old man in a nursing home. But he also might be some crazy stalker.

Kate logged out of Chatter and went to Friendlink, glad Nick could not contact her there. She posted a short update, mentioning her new action plan. Within a few minutes, her chat box chimed and popped open.

"An action plan sounds like a great idea to me," Beverly Amos had written. *"You must really be smart."*

Kate replied with a smiley-face emoticon, then typed, *"Not really. I found myself overwhelmed and realized I had to make some adjustments in time management. Now, if I can just stick with it!"*

"I'm sure you can. You seem to be a very intelligent and gifted young woman. I could learn a lot from your example."

"I bet you are a fine crafter!"

"Well, I try, but I'm not very good. Which leads me to ask you something, if I may."

There was a long pause after Kate read this, and she realized Beverly was waiting for her permission.

"Certainly. Ask. I hope I have an answer."

"It's just this. Do you have a pattern for a baby blanket? I'd like to make something for my newest grandbaby, but all the patterns I've found are either too hard or too easy. If you have something that's cute but not too challenging, I'd appreciate it."

An image of a baby afghan she'd designed and crocheted a couple of years ago popped into her mind. A delicate shell pattern with picot edging would be simple but lovely.

"I have just the thing. The pattern is saved on my computer,

and can email it to you, if you'd like. But I thought you didn't have any children."

"LOL. I meant my neighbor's grandbaby. I like to pretend she's mine too. Yes, please email me the pattern. I'll send you my email address in just a bit. My teapot is whistling right now, and the oven timer is going off to let me know my cookies are baked."

"Tea and cookies. Sounds great. Enjoy! And I'll send you that pattern when I get your email address."

"Thanks."

Kate closed the chat box and scanned her Friendlink page, reading updates from friends and followers. She didn't have many yet, but if she worked her plan, that number would grow. She wished she had an update from Vanessa, but she knew her daughter was in the throes of first-year college classes and socializing with her friends. Calling Vanessa wasn't always the best option because Kate did not want to interrupt classes or study time. Often, her calls simply went to voice mail, and that was almost worse than not talking to her daughter at all.

Moms sometimes move down on the list of priorities, Kate thought, and tried not to let it make her feel old and dull.

She received another message from Beverly. This one contained her email address and an effusive "thank you" for Kate's time and kind attention.

Kate opened her email account, wrote a brief note assuring Beverly she would be happy to answer questions if the woman had any difficulty, and attached the pattern. She pressed the Send button and then logged off the Internet.

Ten

By the last Monday in October, Kate had settled into a fairly smooth routine. She found it helped if she showered, dressed, and did her hair and makeup first thing after breakfast. Somehow, going through this routine solidified the notion of "going to work," even if that meant stepping into the small spare room in her house.

One thing she had to be careful of, though, was getting too involved in her chats with Beverly. The older woman was engaging and warm, sharing about her life, and expressing interest in Kate's endeavors. She had traveled a lot, but when her husband developed cancer and passed away, her yen for travel faded.

"These days I'm just a homebody," Beverly had written that morning. *"I like my own little house better than I ever thought I could like living in one place."*

"That's so nice," Kate had replied. *"I wasn't sure I could adjust to life in Texas after living in Maine, but I find the warmer weather and dry climate a novelty that I'm enjoying."*

"I used to have family near El Paso. Do you live near there?"

"No, I'm pretty close to Fort Worth."

"A city girl now, are you?"

"LOL. Not exactly. I'm not sure I'm cut out to be a city girl; that's why I like Sage Hills so much."

They chatted a few more minutes; then, as usual, it was Kate who broke off the conversation with a promise to chat another day.

Just a few minutes later, as Kate was pouring herself a glass of tea, Adam called. "Are you sitting down?" he asked. She could hear the smile in his voice.

"Just a minute and I will be." She pulled out a dining chair and perched on the edge of the seat. "OK. I'm sitting. What's up?"

"Great news!" He paused dramatically. "We have a contract with Brighton & Craig Publishing for *Elegant and Wearable Crochet.*"

She nearly dropped her tea.

"And not only that, but if you are agreeable, they want an entire series, two books a year for the next five years. If they do as well as Alexus thinks they will, she's thinking about a companion series, something simpler for beginners. Looks like this is really going to take off big-time, Kate. I believe within a year, your name will be on the lips of every crocheter in the country."

If Kate had not been sitting, her legs would have folded beneath her. Lately, as she spent hours building her collection and following Adam's recommendations, she had begun to believe she could have a modest career doing what she loved. But to the extent he now predicted?

"Oh my," she said weakly, closing her eyes.

His warm chuckle rolled through the phone.

"You aren't going to faint, are you? Do I need to come over there with some smelling salts, or maybe a cold cloth for your head?"

She laughed, but it sounded more like the chittering of a nervous squirrel. She pressed one hand against her chest and felt the rushing thrum of her blood.

"I ... I just don't know what to say."

"Say that you are going to put on a fresh pot of coffee and

serve me something I probably shouldn't eat. I'm bringing this contract to you, and we'll go over it, point by point."

"Now?"

"Right now."

Thank goodness I'm dressed for work. She made a hurried trip to Murray's Market a few blocks away and purchased some Danish for celebration.

With the contract read, signed, and in its manila folder, Adam and Kate drank their second cups of coffee and ate the Danish. It tasted so good, she helped herself to a second piece. Adam patted his stomach and turned down an extra serving.

"I try to limit my treats. Really I do, but what fun is life if you can't eat or drink something you're not supposed to from time to time?"

"Exactly. Just don't overdo it." Kate covered the rest of the Danish and stashed it in the refrigerator, out of sight.

"Adam," she said when she sat back down, "I've been looking at crochet blogs and websites, and I'd like to spiff mine up a bit from a simple blog. What do you think?"

"My dear," Adam patted her hand in the most fatherly way, "I think that sounds fine, but why not hold off on that for a little while." He paused, then added, "We don't want anything to distract you from your actual design time. In fact, don't let any of the online networking compromise your time. Some of it is necessary, of course, because you need to build a loyal following. However, your fans will connect with you and demand a lot of your time and attention if you aren't careful. I believe Alexus Lauren will be able to suggest some ways for that not to happen. Stretching one's self too thin can lead to burnout. We don't want that for you. Over time, the publishing company might choose to take over all official social media for you.

I'll do my best to encourage Alexus to that end. Maybe it can happen sooner rather than later."

Adam was so kind, and that fatherly touch awakened a yearning in Kate she had suppressed for years. Her parents had divorced when Kate was young. Like so many children of divorce, Kate was raised by her mother and had little contact with her father. Maybe that was one reason she was drawn to Adam. He was quickly becoming a father figure in her life, an older and wiser man who looked at her as a person, not as a potential date or conquest.

"Kate?" he said, almost as if he was reading her mind. "Do you have something on your mind?"

She took in a deep breath and let it out. "Yes," she said, before she overthought the moment. "Yes, I do, and I probably should tell you about it."

Adam's dark eyes filled with concern and his gaze never wavered from her face. "Tell me."

She told him about her history with Nick, then added, "He is now following me on Chatter."

"Is he making threats?"

"No. He's just being annoying, filling my feed with a constant stream of comments. Look—" She got her laptop and logged onto the site. "There they are. And there is even more now."

Adam scrolled through, reading, frowning, grimacing. At last he heaved a huge sigh and turned to Kate. "What do you want to do?"

"What can I do? I want him to leave me alone."

Adam turned back to the screen then tapped a few keys. "Look. We can do this. Do you want to?"

She read, "Block @NickScott's chatter."

"Yes!" she said. "I didn't realize I could block chatter buddies."

Adam smiled at her. "Just takes a little know-how, that's all. Some of these sites aren't as easy to navigate as you might think." He clicked the Agree button, and the words "@NickScott can no longer chatter on your feed" popped up.

"Wonderful," she said, smiling, feeling so much relief that her body felt twenty pounds lighter. "Thank you."

"Kate," he said, his face serious again, "you have such a sweet and trusting nature. Please be careful when making friends with people online. Not everyone is as open and honest as you are; not everyone should be trusted."

"I know. I have come to realize that, and believe me, this experience with Nick has taught me a valuable lesson."

"What about other online friends?"

"I have a few, of course. None that I chat with regularly like I did with Nick, but there are a few I exchange crochet talk with." She paused. "Well, that's not exactly accurate. I chat with Beverly quite a bit. She's great. She's older, an eager crafter, a lot of fun to share crochet stories with."

That fatherly expression remained on Adam's face. "Just be careful, Kate. That's all I ask. Don't take anyone at face value."

The cynical approach was hard advice to swallow, but she knew Adam was right. All her life, Kate had been far too trusting, too easily believing the best of everyone. Yes, she was working hard to change herself, but she did not want to swing too far the other way and become hard, suspicious, and cynical.

"I'll be extra careful," she promised.

"Great!" Adam said. "You keep that attitude so you don't get caught in someone's ugly web."

To get the conversation off such a creepy topic, Kate said, "What about this companion book series you mentioned?"

"That's something you and Alexus need to discuss. But not for a while yet. Let's focus on *Elegant and Wearable* first."

She shivered a little. "I'm so excited! But I can't help but remember that mess with Stefan Betrugen. It nearly got Vivi and me killed, for goodness' sake!" She shivered again as the memory wrapped around her. Betrugen, her first publisher, was a crook who had tried to swindle her out of her designs. He had been found dead, and Kate had been the prime suspect until she, Vivi, and Peter had cleared her name. "I don't want that to ever happen again."

"That's in the past," he said softly. "We've all learned from that situation, and we'll do our best to prevent it from ever happening again. Brighton & Craig is a top-notch, well-known company. They've been around a long time. We have every reason to trust them."

She closed her eyes, shoving away the memories.

"You're right, Adam." She opened her eyes, straightened her spine, and lifted her chin. She offered him a smile. "Onward and upward, as the saying goes."

After Adam left, Kate checked her pantry and refrigerator and decided it was time to stock up at the large grocery in Fort Worth. She preferred shopping at Murray's in Sage Hills. It had a hometown feel to it that reminded her of Magruder's back in Stony Point, and that warmed her heart. But, as much as she liked the neighborhood market, for larger shopping forays, she always went to the bigger stores. Wanting to get home before dark, she left right away.

When she got home and pulled into her driveway, she noticed a newer-model black Ford in the driveway of the Tamblin house. She opened the back of her van, hefted out as many bags as she could haul in one trip and walked a little awkwardly with them toward her front door.

She glanced toward the house next door and nearly jumped back when she saw a rather large man standing at the nearest outside corner of the house, staring at her. She said nothing to him as she hurried to let herself inside. She lowered her bags onto the dining table and cast an uneasy glance toward the kitchen window.

Stop it, she told herself. *He isn't even in your yard. I'm not going to cower every time I see a stranger in this neighborhood.*

She had ice cream and a carton of eggs still in the van. With a firm stride and far more bravery than she actually felt, Kate threw open her front door and strode out to retrieve the last of her groceries. A glance next door proved the man was nowhere to be seen. She breathed easier.

She always overthought everything too much. Harry used to yell at her when she'd ponder instead of act. What he never realized was that his yelling only caused her decision making to take longer. Sometimes she wondered if she'd be so timid now if she had never met Harry.

Of course, if I'd never met Harry, I wouldn't have Vanessa. She's the best thing that ever happened to me, so I'm glad Harry and I were married. And now I'm glad we aren't.

She put away her groceries, then scrubbed a large potato at the sink to bake. Her glance wandered next door. The man stood near the house next door, but he was facing her, staring straight at her when she looked up. She dropped the potato with a thud into the stainless steel sink and stepped back out of view, her heart skipping more beats than was comfortable.

How long has he been there?

She waited for a bit. Then, with all the stealth she could muster, Kate edged forward to peep out the window. He was gone. Her breath rushed out, but she was still frightened. With hands wet from washing the potato, she closed the blinds, then rushed through the rest of her house, doing the same. She checked the doors and windows. She'd done the same thing when she first saw Frieda Mahl casting her spell in the backyard.

"I can't let every little thing frighten me!" she said aloud. What kind of existence was that? And what kind of example did she set for her daughter? Vanessa was just starting life in the adult world. She needed to see her mom forging ahead, fearless and determined. Successful.

The next morning, when Kate logged onto her Chatter account, she found *"@KateStevens is adorable in her pink-and-white jammies."*

Eleven

"What?" she squawked, shooting a panicked look around the room as if she might see the voyeur staring at her where she sat in her pink-and-white checked cotton pajamas. *How would someone know what I am wearing in my own home?*

She followed the chat back to its source and found the handle "@JustMe." She immediately clicked on his profile and found nothing—no photo, no bio. Most Chatter accounts followed lots of others. @JustMe followed only one—her. Was this Nick? But if so, how did he know what she was wearing? How could Nick be spying on her? She had met him online before she left Maine, and he didn't know where she lived, then or now. Obviously, someone else was watching her. But who?

What do I do now?

She reached for her phone, paused for a moment, then picked it up and dialed.

It went straight to voice mail.

"Peter, it's Kate. Can you please call me as soon as possible? Thank you." She wondered if he could hear the tremor in her voice.

She no sooner had hung up the phone when it rang.

"Mom?" Vanessa's voice carried an undercurrent of alarm. Kate's mother-bear instinct kicked into high gear. She stiffened.

"Hi, honey. What's wrong?"

"Who is this Nick Scott that is sending me messages?"

Something cold wrapped around Kate's heart and lungs

in less time than it took to blink an eye. She grabbed the edge of the table.

No! How in the world had he found Vanessa? Had Kate ever mentioned her daughter by name? She was pretty sure she had not.

"Mom? You there?"

"I … I'm here." She paused to moisten her dry mouth. "Vanessa, honey. When did he message you?"

"I got one from him late last night, asking about you. He sent a direct message to my Friendlink account." Kate lifted a trembling hand to her lips as Vanessa spoke. "He said you guys were old friends, but he had lost your phone number and address. I told him very politely to message you the same way he'd messaged me, but he said he wanted to surprise you. When I asked what he meant by that, he said it was a secret. It all seemed so fishy that I didn't give him your phone number or anything." She paused. "He isn't some old boyfriend, is he? Or is he?"

"No! He's not an old boyfriend. Vanessa, if he gets in touch with you again, do not reply. OK? Just … don't."

"Mom! I don't like the sound of your voice. Who is that guy? Has he done something?"

Kate picked her words carefully.

"I don't know him, exactly. Just online. But he's no one that I want in my life, or yours. In fact, block him from your Friendlink account. Do it now."

"You're scaring me. What is going on?"

"Nothing is going on. He's just someone who wants to get to know me better, and I'm not interested. So just do what I say and block him. Ignore him if he ever tries to get in touch with you in any way. OK?"

"I don't like this. Is he some kind of stalker or something?"

"Honey, don't worry. I'm handling it; everything is fine."

There was a long silence before Vanessa said quietly, "I can't believe this is happening, Mom. Not to you."

"Nothing is happening."

"I'm calling you every single day to check on you."

"I'd love to talk to you every day," she said, forcing lightness in her voice, "but you don't have to check on me."

"Let me be the judge of that."

Kate couldn't help but laugh a little at Vanessa's burgeoning voice of authority.

"I'll feel much better if you just put this whole thing out of your mind and concentrate on your studies," she said with as much assurance as she could muster. "I'm fine, I promise you."

Again a lengthy silence.

"I don't like this, Mom. Not one bit. But I'll do my best *if* you promise to take care of yourself. I mean it. You're the only mother I have."

"That's true. I am. And speaking of that, do you need anything? I could send you a little money." She thought of her lean checking account and winced, but she'd live on beans and baloney if she had to, to make sure Vanessa had all she needed.

"Dad sent me a check a couple of days ago."

"He did?"

"He did."

Good for Harry, Kate thought. He never seemed to do much for anyone without it having a direct benefit to him, but the exception to that always was Vanessa. Kate had no doubt about that.

"I'm glad. Spend it wisely, honey."

"You know I will, Mom. Listen, I have to go now, or I'll

be late for chem. But take care of yourself, please. Text me later and let me know you're all right. OK? Promise?"

"Yes. I will. Don't be late for your class. I love you, honey."

"Love you too. And please, be careful. I mean it. Don't get involved with crazy guys. They are never good news." Spoken as if Vanessa had firsthand experience—which Kate knew she didn't.

"Sweetie, I'm not involved with anyone but you, I promise."

They had barely said their goodbyes and cut the connection when Kate's phone rang again.

"Kate, it's Adam." His voice lacked its characteristic bright tone and sounded uncompromisingly somber. "Have you been on your blog site today?"

His brusque manner increased her edginess. Her mind characteristically jumped to responsibility. Had she published her latest post too soon? Had she missed a lot of typos or misspelled something crucial?

"Not yet. I've ... had kind of an unsettling morning." She paused, feeling the dread grow and twist in her stomach. She thought of everything she'd just discovered that morning and suppressed a shudder. "Why?"

"Someone has left a rather ... disturbing comment."

"Oh goodness. It was probably written by that fellow I mentioned to you, Nick Scott. The one we blocked from my Chatter feed. I'm sure he's out to create problems for me." She paused and drew in a deep breath. "Honestly, I've had enough! He has even been in touch with Vanessa."

"Your daughter?"

"Yes!" She had to stop and catch her breath again. "Adam, something else is going on. Someone is spying on me."

"What? Why do you say that?"

Without preamble, the fear, uncertainty, and confusion

over recent events broke the fragile dam she had built around them. She burst into tears.

"Kate? Kate, listen to me. I'm on my way."

She tried to swallow down the sobs, but failed.

"You hang tight, my dear. I'll be there shortly."

Quicker than she thought possible, Adam was at her door, ringing the bell and calling her name. By then, she'd managed to pull herself together.

"Adam, God bless you," she said, giving him a quick hug. "Thank you for coming by, but you didn't have to. I'm all right."

"Uh-huh. That's why you've been crying."

She sniffled, her face growing warm with fresh embarrassment.

"Now, listen to me," Adam said, taking her arm and leading her to the love seat. "You and I have talked more than once about how I am not just an agent to my clients. I wear many hats, you know. Right now, I'm wearing my father hat. So, let's sit down, and you tell me what's going on."

Beneath Adam's calming regard, she was able to gather her resolve. She fetched her laptop and settled back down beside him. The Chatter screen came on. She pointed to it.

"See? Right there."

Adam adjusted the screen and leaned forward to read. A deep frown settled on his face.

"How would this person know I was wearing pink-and-white pajamas unless he was spying on me?"

He shook his head. "Good question. Did you mention the pajamas in any of your updates?"

"No. Never. I keep my updates fairly impersonal, completely superficial."

He ran a gaze around the room, noting the windows. "Do you close the blinds at night?"

"Always. The thought of someone peeking in makes my skin crawl."

Adam looked at her laptop again. "Someone might have hacked into your computer and could be spying on you through the built-in camera."

The very idea made her sick to her stomach, and she pressed her fingers against her mouth.

"You have a small Band-Aid or piece of colored tape?"

She nodded.

"Would you get it for me?"

She brought a box of bandages to him. He took out the smallest size and opened it, then placed it across the tiny lens above her screen.

"That will take care of anyone spying on you from your own computer. And when you aren't using it, close your laptop. If you'd like, when I leave, I'll take it to a fellow I know who loves computers beyond all reason. He'll be able to see if it's been hacked."

"Yes, I'd appreciate that. Thank you, Adam."

"Now, if you'll pull up your blog, you need to adjust the settings to allow you to moderate future comments before they go live."

Her most recent blog post had been short, just as Adam had recommended. She had written about how the beauty of crochet could reflect the beauty of nature, of children, or the soul.

She started to read the comment below it, but Adam interrupted her.

"I hate for you read that, Kate. It's ugly."

She grimaced. "I can take it." She took a deep breath. "Well, here goes."

"You write a great blog, Ms. Stevens," she read, "but you

don't practice what you preach. You pretend to be a good friend, a talented artist, a genuine person, but in reality you're a fraud. You treat your friends as someone beneath you. Your 'art' is nothing more than a messy conglomeration of threads and ideas. Your 'genuineness' is a mask for self-interest. In fact, I'm sure if anyone would care to spend the time investigating your 'art,' they would find that everything you claim to be your own original ideas are copied from those with far more talent than you possess. Do us all a favor and crawl back under your rock."

"Oh my," she said, one hand resting on her throat. "Who would write such hateful things?"

Twelve

"It's signed 'anonymous,'" Adam said. "Cowards never use their names."

"I'm sure it's Nick Scott." She chewed her lower lip. "I haven't been blogging long enough to have created other enemies, have I? And even if I'd been doing it for a decade, my blogs are about crochet! I have *never* written an unkind word about anything or anyone!"

"I know that, my dear," he said quietly.

"Adam ..." She met his eyes, not wanting to voice the fear that seemed to grow tendrils. "Do you think this person on Chatter, this '@JustMe' is Nick?"

"I do. It would be simple enough to open a new account with another email address."

"Yes. I know."

"Have you found any suspicious new friends on Friendlink?"

"None. Thus far, everyone is very nice."

"Are you sure he doesn't know where you live?"

"I never told him. He kept asking for my address and phone number. His ranting really got going when I refused, and so I blocked him from my Friendlink account."

"I know you don't want to hear this, Kate, but in this age of cyberspace and technology, with all of the information we have at our fingertips, it wouldn't be hard for him to find your personal information. If he really wanted it."

She looked at him and her heartbeat felt thick, as though her blood had turned to sludge. She swallowed hard.

"I have to put a stop to this—all of it. Making my life miserable and scaring me, that's one thing. But contacting Vanessa ... that's over the line. I won't let that happen again." She shuddered. "And the fact that he saw me ..." She shuddered again. "Do you think Nick is here in Sage Hills? Do you think he's lurking somewhere, spying on me?"

"Anything is possible. But let's consider some other possibilities, including him hacking into your computer."

She nodded, eager to come up with the answer to this awful situation.

"Have you had any suspicious phone calls or letters?"

"Nothing like that. But hardly anyone has my phone number. Ever since Harry and I split up, I've kept a private phone number and only give it out to close friends. I only have a cellphone here."

"Well then, let's look at specific people. Your ex-husband is the first to come to mind. Family members are so close to victims, they are always the first to fall under suspicion. Especially ex-spouses," Adam said. "Do you two get along? Do you think he would do something like this?"

"I hardly think so. Harry is narcissistic and hot-tempered, and he's not a very admirable person. But if he wanted to cause trouble, he'd just create havoc instead of skulking around like an underhanded snake in the grass. Besides, there's nothing in it for him, and if there's nothing in it for Harry, it isn't worth his time."

"What about his friends?"

She shrugged. "I've never met any of the friends he has now. We haven't moved in the same circle for years."

"I see. Then maybe someone in the neighborhood? Who do you think might have means and opportunity to be spying on you?"

A chill ran over her at the mere thought of someone peeking into her windows.

"I know Vivi across the street, and I've spoken to a few of my other neighbors, but I really haven't gotten to know them. Honestly, Adam, I shut my blinds as soon as the sun starts to set."

"I hate to tell you this, my dear, but it doesn't take a very large gap in the blinds or tiny hole in the curtains for someone to see inside."

She winced, knowing he was right.

"Actually, there is someone ... or, was. Yesterday." She turned her gaze to the window that faced the house next door. "A strange man. He was just staring at me, watching me when I came home from the store. And then a little later, I looked out the kitchen window and there he was again, looking this way."

"Peeping in your windows?"

"Not exactly. He was standing over there by the house next door, but staring right at me. I was standing at the kitchen sink. The house has been for sale. I don't know if he has bought it or not."

Adam's frown deepened further. "Did you say anything to him?"

"No."

He sighed heavily and stroked his jaw as he seemed to ponder the situation. "Who else might peek in your windows?"

"I don't know. I haven't lived here long enough to know very many people."

"Still, it doesn't take long to catch someone's attention."

"True," she said, nodding. "Well, there's Frieda."

"Frieda? Who's that?"

"Frieda Mahl. She lives two doors down. And she was

digging in the backyard of that empty house next door—at least two times that I saw her. In the middle of the night."

Interest spread across his face. "In the middle of the night? When was that?"

"The first time was just a couple of weeks ago, but I hadn't been sleeping well, and decided that maybe I had just imagined it. But then it happened again, and I called the police."

Adam nodded. "As you should have done."

"You'd think so, wouldn't you?" she said with considerable irritation. "They showed up, and that was about all they did. The one cop who showed up looked around, and then he told me he found nothing and to go back to bed. Frieda yelled at me for calling the cops on her."

"You called the cops on her?"

She shook her head. "She just happened to be the one who was digging, but I didn't know that at the time."

"Why was she digging in someone else's backyard, and in the middle of the night?"

"Apparently she put together an 'eye of newt and horn of toad' concoction and buried it so the perfect person would buy the house next door."

The expression on Adam's face made her laugh in spite of her unease.

"Vivi—my good friend and neighbor across the street—told me that Frieda fancies herself to have 'powers.' She's odd, and she might peek in windows, but I don't think she'd write a vicious anonymous letter. In fact, she seems the type to come right to my door and yell in my face."

Adam didn't seem to think the notion was as humorous as Kate did.

"I see. But people do peculiar things. Never underestimate

the power to misjudge what a person might do. Someone like Frieda might be trying to cause trouble."

"Gosh, Adam, I'd hate to be so cynical."

He smiled and patted her hand. "Sometimes you have to temper a trusting nature with a good dose of skepticism."

"Well, I doubt Frieda has a computer, and even if she did, I doubt very much she'd interact online, even to cause trouble."

"We need to find out," he said.

"Huh! I guess we can try."

"Leave no stone unturned, my dear. Now, what about this neighbor you mentioned, Vivi?"

"What about her? You mean, Vivi as someone who'd be stalking me online? No, of course not."

"As you said, you don't know anyone here very well yet. What do you know about the woman?"

"Why, I know that she's a good person. She has a sound business head on her shoulders. She loves her mother. And ... and ... she keeps her house clean!"

Both his eyebrows went up, and a slight smile curled his lips. She flushed, waving one hand impatiently. "You know what I mean. She's a decent person, and she cares about people. I just can't believe Vivi would try to harm my career by pretending to be someone else and spreading vile rumors."

But in the back corner of her mind, she knew Adam had a point. She didn't really know that much about Vivi. And how could she be sure that what the woman had told her these last few weeks was the truth?

"What about someone in Maine? Do you know of anyone back there who might have decided to stalk you? A man who might have expressed an interest you didn't return? Or possibly a crafter who is jealous of your talent?"

"No." Once again, though, the soft whisper of doubt prodded her with unease. "Stony Point is a small, close-knit town, and I didn't have enemies there."

"OK," he said after a minute. "But, Kate, I want you to think about this. Try to come up with someone, anyone, you think would try to cause problems for you. Make a list of everyone you know, suspect or not."

"I will."

"And if you come up with anything at all—"

She nodded. "I'll call you."

"Me, yes. But call the police too. You may have to build a case against someone, so it's better if you can document as much as possible."

Her stomach was in knots, but she nodded again. "I will, but the Sage Hills police don't seem to be very interested. I think they think I'm crazy."

"I've heard there are a couple of macho-men types with the local police force. If they give you trouble, call their sergeant."

"I'll call Peter Mathews. You remember him, don't you? He's a police detective in Fort Worth, and you met him at the party Paige held a few weeks ago."

Adam grinned. "I remember him. The way your eyes sparkle when you say his name, I assume this fellow is more than just a detective."

Her face grew warm, but before she could reply, her cellphone rang.

"Hello, Kate. It's Peter. I just got your message."

Kate couldn't help the sweet rush of relief that swept through her. She pointed at the phone and mouthed Peter's name to Adam. He gave her a thumbs-up.

"Hi. I'm so glad you called back."

"What's up? Are you fixing me dinner tonight? Are you

asking me to go to a movie? What about a ride in the moonlight this evening?"

In spite of herself, Kate laughed.

"Adam and I are going over some things, so none of the above for you."

"Adam?"

"Yes. My agent."

"I remember him, but I didn't realize he was your agent. It's great that he is. But I'm heartbroken that you aren't asking me for dinner, a movie, and a drive."

"Yes, I'm sure you are." She sobered. "Actually, I called you about something serious."

"Oh?" She could feel the change come over him.

"It seems someone has been spying on me."

"Spying? What do you mean? Spying how?"

She told him about the disturbing message, and as he probed, she mentioned the strange man who had been at the vacant house next door.

"Do you know this man? Have you seen him before?"

"Not at all, and I'm sure I would have remembered him. But he stared at me so … so oddly. As if he were memorizing my face."

"Did you call the Sage Hills P.D.?"

"Um, yes. But not today and not about him."

A silence crackled briefly through the phone. "When and why did you call them?"

She squirmed. "It was nothing, actually. I mean, I thought it was something, but it turned out to be nothing."

"Kate."

She told him about seeing Frieda digging in the backyard and calling the police about it.

"I feel so silly now," she said.

"Don't. You did the right thing."

"The officer did not take me very seriously."

"Was he an old guy? Acted like you were a pain in the neck, and he'd rather be eating doughnuts?"

"Yes. You sound like you know him."

"I do."

"He said he couldn't find anything. I don't think he looked very hard, because Vivi and I found it."

"Found what?"

"Actually, Frieda stopped me before I'd reached whatever 'charms' she'd buried."

Adam said, "Tell him about Nick."

"What was that?" Peter said. "Tell me about who?"

"There was some guy who made a pest of himself online. That's all. As I said, I've blocked him."

"Tell me more."

"I was chatting with him on Friendlink for a while, and he started getting out of line."

"Out of line how?"

"He wanted my phone number and address. I refused to tell him and he got angry. When he became obnoxious about it, I discharged his friendship. Then he started following me everywhere on the Internet." She pulled in a deep breath. "He got in touch with Vanessa, pretending to be an old friend of mine. She was too smart for him and told him nothing."

"Good for her. Has he made any threats to either of you?"

"No. He just got obnoxious and started sending me scads of emails, filled up my Chatter feed with a lot of nonsense, and posted hateful comments on my latest blog post. At least, I'm pretty sure it was him."

"You're sure he made no threats, even veiled?"

"I'm sure. I feel confident he'll leave me alone when

he realizes I am not going to respond to him." She was proud of how firm and self-assured she sounded as she made this announcement. Now, if she could fully believe what she'd just said.

"OK. I want you to be vigilant about this guy. You and Vanessa both, all right? Let me know if he gets in touch with you again. In any way—online, phone call, letter, in person. In the meantime, delete all your accounts and set up new ones."

"Oh, goodness," she said in dismay, thinking of the time she'd spent setting up those accounts and building a following.

"I care about you, Kate. I don't want anyone to hurt you. Ever." His voice was so quiet when he spoke those words that she barely heard him. In the background lay the sound of voices and ringing telephones. Peter must have been in the precinct and surrounded by co-workers.

"Thank you," she said. Anything else she had planned to say to him flew right out of her head. "Talk to you later, Peter."

"So what did Peter have to say that has you looking like that?" Adam didn't try to hide his grin.

"Looking like what?" She opened her eyes wide as if she had no idea what he meant. "He said I need to delete all my accounts and start new ones."

Adam winced. "Ouch."

"Exactly. I have spent hours organizing, and now …" She frowned. "What do you think, Adam?"

"I think you should listen to Peter. Close down all your accounts. As I said before, I'll talk to Alexus and see if Brighton & Craig can't take over this part."

"All that time I spent on them …."

An expression of gentleness and wisdom settled over his creased features.

"I know. But, listen to me, Kate. Give yourself permission to step back and re-evaluate. Aside from all the years you've spent becoming a fabulous expert in the art of crochet, you are now in those early first steps of your publishing and design career. There are going to be pitfalls and detours. This Nick person is an ugly pitfall, but don't let him detour your progress."

She sagged a little as Adam's gentle words poured over her. "Thank you," she said. "Really, I'm not even going to think about Nick very much. I want to focus on my work."

"That's what I want to hear! And you keep Peter—and me—in the loop concerning all this." He pinned a hard look on her. "All right?"

"Yes. I will." She put the laptop aside and reached into the basket she kept beside the love seat. She took out the evening wrap she had nearly finished and showed it to Adam. "I only need to work in these loose ends and this will be finished. What do you think?"

He took it from her hands, his eyes bright with interest and appreciation.

"Look at that," he said as he pulled it across his fingers. "It's beautiful. That shimmering thread and the stitch technique you've used make it look almost liquid."

"I'm giving it to Vivi. She has been so sweet to me, and I wanted to do something nice for her."

Adam's face creased into a warm smile. "You're a very lovely young woman, Kate."

This time when she blushed, she kept her head up, instead of ducking or turning away. She touched the wrap with her fingertips.

"Since this one is turning out so well, I'll make another to show in Paige's shop. I hope people like it."

"Of course they will, Kate. Soon everyone will want an original Kate Stevens design."

"Oh my," she said, feeling a little light-headed, as she always did when thinking about success on a larger level. "I hope you're right."

"Of course I'm right!" He laughed. "Plus, you'll soon be getting a sizable advance for your book."

She felt her eyes go wide. "I'd forgotten all about that!"

He laughed again, a hearty sound that made her giggle with him. "As your books and designs grow in popularity, your advances will increase in amount. Isn't it good to know that you are able to make a living doing something you love?"

For the first time in several weeks, Kate felt her burden lighten, as if something literally had been lifted from her physical body. She put both hands on either side of her face and smiled so hard she was afraid her cheeks would split. Then she remembered. With recognition also came a loss of her anonymity. Nick Scott might not be the only one who'd want to cause trouble.

Adam returned with her laptop that afternoon. "Good news is, you haven't been hacked. Bad news, there's probably a Peeping Tom in the neighborhood. I stopped at the police station and talked with an officer. They'll keep an eye out. And you, my dear, be vigilant at night."

"I will." She glared at her windows and sighed. "It's so unfair that someone can intrude in another person's life this way."

He touched her arm. "Yes, it is. Stay strong, and call me anytime. All right?"

She smiled and laid her hand on his. "I will. Thank you."

"And I recommend you update Peter too. He obviously cares about you."

As soon as Adam left, Kate called Peter.

"Thanks for letting me know, Kate. I appreciate Adam looking out for you. He's a good guy to have in your corner."

She smiled at how each man had praised the other in this situation. She was lucky to have both of them in her life.

"I'll call a couple of buddies of mine in the S.H.P.D. and ask them to beef up patrol in your neighborhood," Peter said. "In the meantime, you be careful."

"I will."

When she ended the call, she deleted all her online accounts. It only took a few minutes, far less time than she had devoted to creating and building them. She set up a new email account, but planned to use it only for a few select friends. Taking Adam's advice, she set aside social media and networking. From this point on she planned to put all her energy into her passion, which was crochet and design. Her editor at Brighton & Craig might have other ideas, but at that moment, Kate was doing what she felt was best.

My action plan is toast, she thought. *I'll come up with a new one another day.*

That evening, Vivi showed up bearing two large takeout boxes of Tex-Mex food.

"I hope you haven't eaten," she said the moment Kate opened the door. "These are the best chimichangas in Fort Worth. Maybe in all of Texas."

"That's saying something," Kate said, grinning. "Come inside."

Vivi took the food from the sacks as Kate took a pitcher of tea out of the refrigerator and two glasses from the cabinet.

"I have gained twelve pounds since you walked in the

door, and I haven't taken a bite yet," Kate declared. She filled the glasses with ice and poured the tea. Then both women settled down at the table. "Thank you, Vivi. This is so great."

"When Vivi wants Mexican food, Vivi gets Mexican food."

They piled their plates high with succulent deep-fried chimichangas, spicy Spanish rice, mellow refried beans, cool guacamole, and mounds of fresh lettuce, tomatoes and onions. They ate with gusto and laughter. Finally full, Kate tenderly rubbed her stomach and gave a mock groan. "I don't think I can move."

Vivi laughed. "Me either. But do you think we can at least stagger out to the patio for some fresh air? It might help revive us."

Kate's gaiety faltered at the thought of going out into the twilight. Full darkness would encompass the landscape in a few minutes, and she had no desire to be in it.

"Let's stay inside." She shot a look toward the windows, then turned her eyes to Vivi. "I'm glad you came over because I have something to tell you. I could have called or sent you a text, but I didn't want to spook you on your way home."

Vivi grew completely still. "I don't understand."

"We seem to have a peeping tom in the neighborhood."

"What?" Vivi's eyes grew big.

"Someone left a comment about me and my pajamas on Chatter. I don't know who it was, but apparently someone peeked in my windows."

"Oh, my word!" Vivi looked toward the windows. The blinds were closed and curtains pulled. "How did he see inside?"

"I don't know. I've tried to smooth and straighten all the window coverings so that there isn't any way for anyone to peep in, but as Adam said, you don't need a very big hole to be able to see."

Setting her mouth in a grim line, Vivi huffed loudly. "Well, I have a marble rolling pin, and I'm not afraid to use it." There was a brief silence, then she added, "Of course it won't keep someone from looking in the window. But if he were to come inside the house ... *blam!*"

The next day, Kate drove to Sage Hills Sports and More and perused baseball bats. She hefted several until she found one that felt right in her hands.

Blam! she thought as she carried it to the cash register.

"A little late in the year for softball," the young clerk behind the counter said.

"Yes, it is." She did not bother to tell him she was purchasing the bat for other purposes.

Vivi has her marble rolling pin, and I have a Louisville Slugger. We're quite a pair.

After she got home, Kate changed into jeans and a long-sleeved T-shirt and spent some time working outside. She was in the front yard, deadheading the mums, when a dark blue Lincoln pulled into the driveway next door. "M.J. Cardwell Realty" was emblazoned on the side in large, glittering, gold letters. The luxury car looked out of place in the modest, middle-class neighborhood, and its size diminished the single-car driveway and simple carport.

The driver and a passenger sat talking in the front seat as Kate's curiosity ate at her. Could it be she was going to get a new neighbor? If so, she hoped it was someone as friendly and likable as Vivi Lawrence. Having someone next door would even add a measure of security. She continued to work on her plants and tried not to stare too openly when both front car doors finally opened.

The driver was a tall, buxom woman in a blood-red blazer, black slacks, and stiletto heels. Her dark hair was piled into a tower of stiff curls. They stood, each near the open door from which they'd emerged, and looked at the house. The agent's strong voice came across the yard in the quiet air of early afternoon: "You could get this for a song, I'm sure. It's been vacant for quite some time."

The man's quiet voice did not carry to Kate. The pair moved away from the car and walked toward the house. That was when Kate saw the man fully. A chill crept across her scalp and down her back. She recognized him immediately as the man she had seen at the house two days earlier. Average to tall, older, burly, with thinning brown hair, he wore a short-sleeved blue plaid shirt and nondescript jeans. As if sensing her attention, he turned and looked straight at her.

He said something to the agent, and she glanced over her shoulder at Kate. The wide, bright smile stretched her cheeks and never left her face.

"Let's go meet her," the woman sang out. They changed directions and walked toward Kate.

"Hello!" The woman held out a hand heavily laden with rings of every stone and metal. Kate wondered how she could possibly write or use her phone—or even drive—with so many rings and such long fingernails. "Tamara Grant, realtor with M.J. Cardwell Realty. I'm showing Joe this lovely home, and I'm sure it's going to fit his needs exactly." She turned her toothy smile on the man who stared hard at Kate.

"I'm Kate Stevens." She felt wary, but refused to be timid. "I believe I saw you the other day, didn't I?"

He turned his head slightly and leaned forward a bit. "How's that?"

She repeated her question. He smiled, transforming his face from grim intensity to something warmer and kinder.

"Yes, I think you did. My son and I were driving by when we spotted this place." He glanced at the house behind them. "It's perfect for our needs. I'm Joe Vestal." His hand was firm and dry against hers. He seemed about to say something, hesitated a moment, then said, "I think I might have frightened you the other day. Did I? I surely didn't mean to."

"Why, Joe!" Tamara brayed. "How could you scare anyone?" She looked at Kate. "He's just a big ol' teddy bear!"

"Actually, you did frighten me a bit," Kate said.

"Mercy." Tamara rested one hand on her chest. "What did you do, Joe?"

"It's my cataracts," he said.

"What?" Tamara asked.

"I have cataracts, so it's hard for me to see clearly. Unfortunately, I have to squint and stare, trying to make out details. I've been told I look rather off-putting when I do that, but I'm at the point glasses can't help me, so I do what I must to be able to see. Mrs. Stevens, I really do apologize."

"Oh goodness," Kate sighed. Obviously he had hearing problems too. Shame filled her as she remembered how suspicious she'd been of this poor fellow.

"It's a good thing you have me right here to show you this house." Tamara tucked her arm in his. "Let's go look at it, and I will tell you all the details your poor eyes cannot." She glanced at Kate. "So nice to meet you, Kate."

"Thank you. Goodbye," Joe said as he allowed himself to be pulled away.

"Goodbye," she said.

"Oh, this isn't goodbye, I'm sure," Tamara said over her shoulder. "It's more like 'hello, neighbor!'"

Joe looked back at Kate, nodded and smiled.

As Kate watched them walk toward the front door of the other house, she pondered Frieda's buried charms. Not for a moment did Kate believe in charms and magic, but maybe Frieda had been right. Maybe Kate shouldn't have monkeyed with the mojo.

Thirteen

Without the burden of building and maintaining her online presence, Kate joyfully focused on creating designs during most of her daylight hours, leaving little time for leisure. Besides, for Kate, crochet *was* leisure. It fulfilled her and both stimulated and comforted her.

At night, she worked feverishly to make wearable, elegant garments that could not be found anywhere else. The work helped to keep her fear under control, but she remained vigilant, listening for any movement outside her windows. By the following Monday, Kate had completed the second evening wrap and crocheted several pairs of slippers and delicate lace gloves.

"I love these," Paige told her that morning when Kate brought in the items. "You can see I have sold nearly everything you've brought to me so far. You are getting quite a fan base in Fort Worth." Paige glanced up from examining the gloves. "Why, look at you, Kate, blushing to the roots of your hair! You should be proud of yourself, not embarrassed."

She laughed a bit at herself. "I'm not embarrassed. Well, not exactly. It's just that I've always been averse to attention."

"Well, get used to it, hon. You're going to be getting a lot of it."

"That's what Adam says. I have to admit the mere thought turns my knees to gelatin."

"Of course it does, but it comes with the territory."

"I know, but still ..." Kate wrinkled her nose.

Paige smiled at her.

"I believe you are on your way. Adam told me about the book contract. I am more impressed than I can say."

"Thank you."

A young woman with light brown hair hanging past her shoulders approached the counter, and Paige turned to her.

"May I help you?"

The girl gave her a nervous smile and shook her head. She stared for a moment at Kate, then moved away, but stayed within a few yards, mulling over a display of needles, muslin, and embroidery floss. Paige met Kate's eyes and made a silent signal with a small shrug of her shoulders.

"You've brought a portfolio, I see," Paige said, turning her attention to the brown leather case Kate held. "Something I can look at, I hope?"

"Yes. I want to get your feedback on these designs." Kate laid the portfolio on the counter and opened it.

"Why, my goodness!" Paige looked as pleased as if Kate had given her a gift. "I'd be so honored."

For the next hour—interrupted by phone calls and customers—the two of them stood at the counter, going over Kate's sketches. The odd young woman approached from time to time, stretching and straining her neck, trying to see the sketches from a distance until Kate or Paige would look up and notice her, and then she'd drift away again.

"What's with her?" Kate whispered.

"I have no idea, but she's freaking me out a little."

They looked at the girl again, but she turned her back and seemed engrossed in a pair of knitting needles.

"I hope she isn't a shoplifter," Paige whispered. "Excuse me, Kate." She stepped out from behind the counter, but when the young woman saw her approach, she quickly headed outside. Paige went to the door and watched her.

"She's gone out of sight," she said. Paige studied the area where the girl had been browsing. "I don't see that anything is missing." She shrugged and returned to her place behind the counter. "Well, there are all kinds of people in the world. Now, which one of these designs did you say is your favorite?"

"I like them all, of course, but I think this one could be the most versatile. Look at the bodice," Kate said, tapping her forefinger against the drawing of a luxurious evening gown. "I'm playing with the idea of making a version with it fitted, and another with it loose, almost blousy. What do you think?"

Paige studied the design, eyes narrowed in thought. Kate clearly saw that Paige did not have the inner eye of a designer, so she picked up a pencil and sketched quickly.

"Like this." She pushed the image across the counter.

Paige's eyes lit up. "Yes. With a long, slim skirt, the bodice would look lovely either way. Or even a flowing long skirt."

"Yes. A small train, one that's barely there. Wouldn't that be lovely?"

"Kate, you're so clever," Paige sighed. "Giving customers a choice is a great idea. Make one of each and I'll display them. In fact, I'll display something of everything in this portfolio."

"Perhaps if the publisher would agree to get a photographer in here, the photos could accompany the patterns in the book."

"Yes. And oh, Kate, how about a fashion show?" Paige's eyes shone with excitement.

Kate remembered the previous fashion show in which

she was involved and felt a moment of panic. "As long as I don't have to model anything, I love the idea."

"Oh, honey, you have the figure for fashion," Paige said, her tone a bit wheedling. But Kate shook her head vigorously.

"Never."

The two women regarded each other for a moment, then burst out laughing. "OK, you win," Paige said. "We can get some of the girls from Regency College maybe."

"Vanessa is making a lot of friends there. I bet they'd be happy to be a part of it. And maybe your daughter too?"

"I think Cheri would be over the moon to participate."

"I'll do it, then," Kate said. She glanced at the clock. "I need to go. We've discussed so much, and I have a lot to get done." She slid her sketches back into the portfolio and closed it. Clasping it to her chest, she said, "This is my beloved treasure trove, and I keep adding more."

Paige eyed the portfolio.

"Do you have copies of the designs that you could leave with me? I'd really like to study them again, maybe tonight at home."

"I don't have copies. Sorry."

"Too bad," Paige said. "But I understand."

Kate drove to Adam's apartment, her brain bursting with more ideas than she could possibly design in a year. She began filling him in almost before he opened the door. He led her to the table and poured her a glass of icy sweet tea.

"Well, well. You are going to be busy." He sat down across from her.

"Yes," she said, "and I have been busy all this time, but

it's so good to have goals, isn't it? Something to strive for." She sipped her tea, then told him about Paige's idea of a fashion show.

"That is an excellent idea. We'll try to get some of the local TV stations to cover it—make sure the newspapers get a press release."

"My goodness," she said, leaning back in her chair. "I feel as though I've run twenty miles today."

"I'm sure you do." He stroked his jaw, eyes narrowed, looking at her. "Maybe you should actually take up running with me. It's a grand way to keep your stress level down, and it's good for you."

Add running to her list of things to do? She laughed. "I'll think about it." She sipped her tea. "Oh, and I nearly forgot to tell you. Remember the strange man I mentioned who was staring at me from the house next door?"

Adam frowned slightly. "What about him? Is he back?"

She made a fluttery gesture. "I'm so embarrassed. He returned with a real estate agent last Wednesday, and I think he might turn out to be my new neighbor."

Adam's frown deepened. "I don't like that, Kate. A Peeping Tom—"

"Oh, he's not a Peeping Tom," she said hurriedly. "I overreacted. The poor fellow has cataracts, and he was just squinting and staring, trying to see."

"To see in your windows?"

"No! Well, I don't know what he was looking at, but if he's as blind as he says, then he did not see me at all when I was standing at the sink. He was just looking toward my house."Adam did not seem convinced. "Remember you told me that you're going to be more careful who you trust from now on? That includes half-blind neighbors."

"Don't be so cynical."

He stirred an extra pack of sweetener into his tea.

"Better cynical than ... something else." He gave her a sharp look over the rim of the glass.

She met his gaze. "Don't worry, Adam. You're talking to the new and improved Kate."

"There was nothing wrong with the old one, as far as I'm concerned. But whichever one you are, just be careful."

On her way home, Kate stopped at MegaFood and ran inside to pick up a few groceries. With her mind so full of ideas and plans, she picked up the items almost by rote, barely noticing what she bought. At home, she unloaded the few bags from the backseat and carried them into the house, then returned to get her portfolio. Usually, if she took it anywhere, she kept it on the front seat, where she could retrieve it easily. But it was neither in the front nor the back. She looked beneath the seats and found nothing. She dropped to her knees and looked beneath the van. Nothing.

Her mind had been so busy that day, focused on her plans and ideas. Maybe she had tossed it in the cargo area without thinking. She scrambled to her feet and hurried to look, but it was not there either. She retraced her steps to and from the door and walked around the yard, probing every inch with her gaze. Inside the house, she sought the portfolio in every room, even though she had only been in the living room and kitchen since she returned home. The portfolio simply was nowhere to be found.

She dug her cellphone out of her purse and called Adam.

"Did I leave my portfolio in your apartment?" she blurted the moment he picked up.

"No, you took it with you. I remember watching you replace all your sketches with such care and thinking how much you loved your work. You didn't lose it, did you?"

"Oh, Adam," she all but wailed, "I can't find it anywhere. I stopped at the market to pick up a few things after I left your place, but I didn't take it inside with me. And it's just gone."

"You went straight from my apartment to the store, right? No stops anywhere in between, not even to the post office for stamps or somewhere for a cappuccino? Nothing like that?"

"Nothing. Straight to the store, straight home. No stops, except at stoplights."

"Did you look around outside the car, in case it fell out?"

"Yes! Everywhere. Well, except at the market, of course. I didn't know it was missing then. I'll go back. Maybe someone found it and turned it in."

"Did you lock your van?"

"I always lock it. Even in Stony Point, I locked it."

"Maybe it fell out there. Someone surely has turned it in. Go see, and then let me know if you find it."

She drove back to the market, her mind spinning with worry. She imagined the clasp of her portfolio broken, sketches scattered like dry autumn leaves all over the parking lot, torn and marked with tire tracks.

What if, just this once, she'd neglected to lock her van? Maybe someone saw the designer leather case in her front seat as she was shopping and snatched it. The sketches would be nothing to them, and they probably threw them away. She felt sick as the vision played itself out in her mind. She should have covered the portfolio with something, or hidden it somewhere in her vehicle.

The parking lot was only about half full, and no car filled the space she'd used earlier. She drove slowly, her gaze scouring every inch of the paved lot, looking for loose papers and brown leather. Seeing nothing, Kate wasn't sure whether to be relieved or despairing. At least if the papers had scattered, she could have gathered them up.

She hoped someone had seen her portfolio and turned it in rather than opening it and keeping it or throwing it in the trash.

In the trash!

She parked near a trash can and rushed to it. All she found there were fast-food wrappers, discarded bags, and a multiplicity of cigarette butts. She ran to the next trash can halfway across the lot. Scrabbling through the garbage, she caught the attention of shoppers passing with carts full of purchases.

A little boy in blue jeans and a red T-shirt pointed at her. "Why is that woman playing in the garbage?"

His mother shushed him and hurried past, the wheels of her shopping cart rattling like rocks in a wheelbarrow. Her upper lip curled in disgust as she eyed Kate. Kate would have waded through a sludge of grape jelly and ketchup to get to her sketches. She ignored the stares and kept searching.

She was scrounging in the last receptacle when a voice startled her. "Are you looking for something, ma'am?"

She turned to see a hefty, red-faced man in a white shirt, brown tie and tan slacks. His rosy neck bulged over the tight collar. His face ran with perspiration.

"Yes, I am! My sketches." She returned to her pillaging.

"Perhaps I can help you, ma'am, but please don't pick through the trash."

Kate shot a glance his way. "I have to go through this trash, in case someone threw my work away."

"Your work?" He stepped closer. He smelled strongly of sweat and cheap after-shave. "Ma'am, please stop pilfering. We can't have customers seeing someone scavenge the garbage in front of our store, you understand."

"You *don't* understand. I've lost my sketches, all my designs. They were in a brown leather portfolio about this big." She measured with her hands. "I had it in my van when I stopped here about forty-five minutes ago, and when I got home, it was gone."

"Did you look in your vehicle?"

"That was the first place I looked. Under the seats, behind them, in the back, anywhere something could be."

"Did you look in your house?"

She huffed. "Yes! But the portfolio didn't make it to my house. This is the only place I stopped. Somewhere between here and my house, it went missing."

He scratched the back of his neck, then wiped a palm down his sweaty face.

"Ma'am, I don't know what to tell you other than you can't dig through our trash."

Knowing her sketches were in none of the receptacles because she'd gone through each of the nasty things, her hands now stinking of ketchup, diet Coke and old greasy fries, Kate straightened. She tried to wipe away the sticky residue on her fingers and stifled a gag when it would not come off. "Believe me, I wasn't digging through your trash for fun."

He blinked his round eyes, then narrowed them, but before he could retort, she said, "Maybe someone turned in my property to your lost-and-found department. You do have a lost-and-found, don't you?"

"Yes ma'am. But no one has turned in anything today."

"Are you sure?"

His pink face got redder. "I am Jimmy Dale Ford, the assistant manager. I have been in the office since we opened, so if someone had turned in anything, I would have known it."

They had collected an audience, and her skin crawled

with embarrassment as well as whatever substances she'd encountered in the trash cans.

You can catch more flies with honey than vinegar. The platitude echoed from Mrs. Bogart's eighth-grade English class. The woman had always been soft-spoken and gentle, but tough. No one ever got away with anything when Mrs. Bogart was on the scene.

Kate closed her eyes and focused on tamping down her anger and frustration. After a moment, she opened them and did her best to give the man a placating smile.

"Please understand," she said quietly, "that portfolio contains months of work. It will cost me dearly if I have lost it. Surely you can understand that I'm upset? I didn't consider store policy when it came to your trash cans. I acted on instinct."

The manager merely looked at her a bit longer, then glanced at the ever-growing crowd they had attracted.

"Folks," he said to the onlookers, a big juicy smile on his face, "we're running a manager's special on soda pop for the next hour. Buy two, get one free. Go get yourself some. A great deal like that, we might run out!" He continued to grin and nod, waving the shoppers toward the store. As soon as they were on their way, his grin slid away. He stepped closer to Kate and lowered his voice. "No one has turned in anything, or I would have known about it. If you left your car unlocked, it's likely someone took your belongings. That's not MegaFood's responsibility. Now, I'm sorry as can be that you lost your portfolio, but I can't have you coming around here, stirring up trouble for our store."

"But—"

"Give me your phone number. If someone turns it in, I'll get in touch. All right?"

His round eyes never wavered from hers, never blinked, never softened.

"Fine," she said with resignation. She scribbled her phone number on a scrap of paper from her purse. "Here."

"Yes ma'am. Now, if that's all I can help you with, I've gotta get back to the store."

As she drove home, Kate pondered every possible event that could have happened to her sketches. The scenario that made her blood run cold was someone claiming the designs as their own. The notion upset her so much, she pulled into the first parking space she saw and sat there, staring at nothing, feeling her energy drain like tepid bathwater down a drain. If anything was a crime, the theft of her sketches certainly was.

She plucked her cellphone from her purse and called Peter.

Fourteen

"How is Kate today?" Peter asked, answering her call almost immediately. She could almost see his warm smile, and her heart quickened.

"Hi, Peter. I'm sorry to bother you, but something terrible has happened."

In the same way she had visualized his smile, she now imagined it slipping away and his expression turning to somber business.

"What's happened?"

"It's my portfolio. The one where I keep all my sketches and design notes. It's gone."

"What do you mean, gone?"

"I think someone took it." She went on to tell him about every step she'd taken up to and including pulling off the street to call him. She described her leather case in detail, right down to the zigzag scratch that she had accidentally put on it during the move to Sage Hills.

"There was a strange woman in Once Upon a Yarn," she said. "She kept hanging on the periphery as Paige and I talked."

"Did you get a good look at her?"

"She was pretty plain. About as tall as me, medium-length light brown hair, jeans and sweatshirt, no makeup. Paige thought she might be a shoplifter, but she didn't take anything."

"What makes you think she took your portfolio?"

"I don't know. She just acted strange, approaching us,

then skittering off when we noticed she was there. It was like she was watching."

"Did you see her around your van?"

"I didn't, and I was parked near the front door. Paige watched her leave the shopping center." She paused. "Even if she had been able to get into my vehicle, she couldn't have taken my portfolio then, because I had it with me in the store."

"Did you lock the doors to your van?"

"Yes, I did. I always lock all my doors."

But had she? In her muddled state of mind, had security slipped her mind this one time?

"Did you notice any signs of entry—broken glass, that sort of thing?"

"Nothing like that."

"I see. What kind of value do you place on your collection of sketches?" he asked.

"Well, I ..." Her voice trailed as she pondered. "Honestly, I'm not sure. They are original designs and no copies exist. I'd never given a thought about making duplicates. I made four copies of a perfectly worthless action plan, but not a single copy of irreplaceable work."

"Don't beat yourself up," he said gently. "Have you reported this to the local P.D.?"

"No. You're the first one I've called. Well, other than Adam. I called him because I thought I might have left the portfolio in his apartment, but I didn't."

"OK, Kate. Talk to the police in Sage Hills. I doubt they'll give the portfolio high priority, but you need to make the report as a matter of record. And don't let them give you the runaround. If they do, let me know. I'll treat this as an official call and will make a report to our department, just in case it happened inside the Fort Worth city limits."

"All right. Thank you so much for taking me seriously."

"Anytime. You know that."

Just as Peter had predicted, the Sage Hills Police Department didn't give her lost property high priority, but at least they took her statement and assured her that if they found the portfolio, someone would be in touch.

She drove back to Once Upon a Yarn. Paige stood behind the counter, head tilted to cradle the telephone, a skein of yarn in one hand, writing busily in a notebook with the other.

"Yes, I understand, but I still need them by the end of next week," she was saying to the party on the other end of the phone call. She looked up as Kate entered and lifted the hand that held the pen in greeting. "Lot number 56S-7821K. Thank you."

She hung up and laid down her pen. "Back again so soon, Kate?"

"Yes. I have a problem."

Paige's eyebrows went up. "Oh? Something I can help you with?"

"I seem to have lost my sketches."

Paige's eyes got big, and she looked horrified.

"Lost them? How?"

"I don't know." She felt tears forming and blinked them back. "When I got home ..." Her voice cracked, and she paused to swallow hard. "When I got home, they were gone."

"My goodness. Kate, you're white as a ghost, honey. Sit down." She ushered her to one of the chairs near the small electric fireplace. She poured her a cup of coffee and put it in Kate's chilly hands.

"Thank you," Kate whispered and sipped. "I just ... I'm so ..."

"What happened?"

"I wish I knew. When I got home, the portfolio was missing. I've looked everywhere. I even went back to the market where I'd stopped earlier for some groceries, and I dug through every trash can in the parking lot."

"Oh my. Well, did you go inside and ask if it had been turned in?"

"The manager said no one had turned in anything. I called Peter, and I reported it to the Sage Hills police, but I doubt that will do a smidgen of good." She sipped the coffee again, enjoying the scalding feel of it on her tongue and down her throat. She needed to feel something other than this awful stone in her heart and belly.

"If you can't find your portfolio, this will set you back several weeks, won't it?"

"Yes, it will, but I'll do my best to knuckle down and sketch the designs again."

"You can do it. I know you can."

Kate smiled and nodded. "I can. But sometimes ... well, the first flush of creativity is gone, and I'm not sure I can re-create them the way they were."

Paige picked up the skein of yarn she'd carried with her when she'd led Kate to the chair. She stared at it, frowning, plucking at a strand.

"I'm sure you can come up with new ones."

"Paige, you remember that woman who was in here earlier, hanging around, trying to look at the designs but pretending she wasn't?"

"She made me uncomfortable."

"Me too. Do you know who she was?"

"I've never seen her before." Paige's eyes narrowed. "Come to think of it, she came in not long after you did, and she followed you when you went over to the worsted wool, then trailed you to the counter. The store isn't that big, and it's not unusual for shoppers to go to the same shelves, but it seemed deliberate, as if she was interested in everything that you were interested in. Do you suppose she might have taken it?"

"I don't know. Could she have followed me all over the store, then to Adam's, then to the market, hoping to swipe the portfolio out of my van? Sounds a little far-fetched, don't you think? And I'm sure I locked up when I went into the store. How could she have gotten in without leaving some evidence of the crime?"

"You never know about some people," Paige said. She moved restlessly and glanced around the room.

"You will keep an eye out for that woman, won't you? Or let me know if you happen to see my sketches anywhere?"

"Try not to worry. If I see the sketches or that strange woman, I'll be sure to call you."

Kate gave her a grateful smile. "Thank you so much. It means a lot to have friends at a time like this." The shop's phone rang and Kate stood to leave. "I better be on my way."

"Let me know the minute you find your portfolio, OK? See you later."

The rest of the day, Kate did her best not to worry about her lost designs, but she felt sick and jittery. When Vivi came over that evening, Kate filled her in.

"What is this world coming to?" Vivi fumed. "Stealing sketches, for goodness sake! What are you going to do?"

"If I don't find the portfolio, I'll start all over again, of course."

"Bless you, Kate. I hope you know that I'll help you in any way I can as soon as this Medical Attorney Assessments and Associations convention ends, but that won't be until Saturday night." She rolled her eyes. "I have to be at the hotel bright and early in the morning to make sure our supplies and services people show up. Four days of it—well, five if you count tomorrow. The last time we hosted this bunch, it was a nightmare. I'm packing some things because I'm pretty sure I'll be staying at the hotel. You know, I love my job. I really do. But there are times ...."

"If anyone can handle it, you can, Vivi Lawrence!"

"And if anyone can re-create a slew of designs that have gone missing, you can do it."

"I'm so glad you're my friend," Kate said, laughing. "You make me feel better just by being you."

Later that evening when Vanessa called, Kate brought her up to date.

"That's terrible, Mom. Why would anyone take your sketches?"

"They probably swiped the portfolio thinking it had money or credit cards or something like that."

"This move to Texas has been filled with chaos," Vanessa said. "Have you heard from that online weirdo again?"

She refused to alarm her daughter by giving her details about the comment on her blog and in her Chatter feed. Vanessa had not seen those updates or she would have called about them.

"It's under control. I have effectively blocked him and deleted all my social media accounts. The only thing I have right now is my new email. You haven't heard from him, have you?"

"No, I haven't, but Mom—"

"Let's put him out of our minds, honey. Instead of worrying, you just think about your classes."

"I will, if you promise to be extra careful."

"I promise!"

"I love you, Mom."

"Aw, honey. I can't ask for anything better than that. I love you too."

Later, comfortable in her favorite chair, she scanned her email. She had a message from Mary Beth and another from Annie Dawson Butler in Stony Point, both catching her up on events and activities going on in their neck of the woods.

She had hoped for an email from Beverly, but found nothing. The woman had not corresponded with her since before Kate changed email accounts the previous week, although Kate had added her to her new contacts and sent her the new address.

"Haven't heard from you in a while," she wrote Beverly in a brief email. *"Hope you're doing well and all is fine. Don't forget to get in touch if you have any questions about that baby afghan."*

Life was surely simpler when a person just used the telephone, she thought. *And good old-fashioned letter writing is nothing to be sneered at.*

If there was one way to keep her mind off her trouble, it was to immerse herself in designing or in crocheting. Right then, she wanted to design. She put away the laptop and got out her sketchpad.

Shortly after noon the next day, Paige called her. "Any news about your sketches?"

"Nothing yet. I have been over every square inch of my house, inside and out, and looked through the van again."

"I'm so sorry this has happened. The reason I called is that I have a letter here that belongs to you."

"A letter? For me?"

"A fellow brought it to the counter this morning. Said he'd found it on the floor back by the baby yarns."

"Well, how on earth? It must have slipped out of my portfolio, I guess, but I don't usually keep letters in there. Who's it from?"

"It is nothing that has been sent through the mail—no stamp, no address, just a plain sealed envelope with your name written on it."

"That's peculiar."

"It is indeed. At any rate, I'll keep it here for you until you come in next time, but I wanted to let you know it's here, in case it was something you were missing."

"I've been sketching all day and could use a little break anyway. I'll be there in a bit to pick it up."

As she ran a comb through her hair, she thought how odd it was that only one thing had slipped out of her portfolio, and odder still that it had not been found until today. She shoved her feet into sneakers, grabbed her purse, and headed out the door. The sunny day wrapped warmth around her the moment she stepped outside. *Now* this *is a reason to like Texas,* she thought. *Back in Maine it could be snowing in early November.*

She locked her door and walked toward the van, but paused when someone called out to her.

She turned and saw the black Ford in the driveway of the house next door. She recognized it as belonging to the man who'd been with the real estate agent the previous week. He stood near his car.

"Hi, neighbor!" he said, waving.

She smiled. "Well, hello again. Your name is Joe, right?"

He smiled. "Yes. Joe Vestal. And you are Kate."

Rather than hollering at each other across the distance of their lawns, she walked toward him. "Have you decided to buy the place?"

He turned his head slightly. "How's that?"

She asked him again, louder.

He nodded, gesturing toward the house. "All mine, signed, sealed, and delivered."

"Wow! That didn't take long."

"It was perfect for our needs, and available for immediate possession."

"Good for you!" She looked past him, taking note once more of the shaggy landscaping and dusty windows. "But you surely have your work cut out for you."

He never took his eyes from her face. "Yes. However, I'm determined. Once I set my mind to having something, I don't stop until it's mine."

"That's one way to be sure you get what you want, isn't it?" A movement at the far end of his house caught her attention. "Is your son or wife here? I'd love to meet them." She tried to glimpse whoever had darted around the corner, out of sight.

"No, not yet."

She brought her gaze back to him. "You don't mean you drove yourself over here? I thought you said you couldn't see well enough to drive."

He blinked. "No, of course I can't. My son is in the house, checking on the plumbing, but my wife isn't here. She'll be joining us before long, I hope. I want to get some loose ends wrapped up and get the house in order before I bring her into it. There is some work to be done, and I want it to be just right for her."

"That's so sweet of you. A lot of men would expect their wives to be the ones to put the house in order. She's lucky to have you, I'd say."

"How's that?"

"I said she's lucky to have you."

His face broke into a huge smile.

Another movement caught her eye. This time she saw Frieda Mahl scurrying across the property line back to her own place. Joe turned his head to follow Kate's gaze.

"Who's that?" he asked.

Frieda paused at her front door, looked over her shoulder, and then dashed into the house.

"That is your other neighbor. Apparently, you are here because of her."

He snapped his head around and gave Kate a sharp look. "How's that?"

Kate explained about the digging, the charm, and Frieda's warning not to dig it up.

"So I assume you are the perfect owner for this house, summoned by Frieda," she concluded with a light laugh.

He chuckled. "Well, I guess I should thank her, shouldn't I?"

"That's up to you. I really don't know her, and she doesn't come out of her house very often. I don't think she likes me very much."

His smile faded. "What do you mean?"

She waved one hand dismissively. "I got off to a bad start with her. She saw me poking around in the backyard—your backyard—trying to figure out what she had been doing back there with all that digging. She became rather agitated."

He frowned. "Did she hurt you, or try to?"

"Oh no. She just yelled and waved her arms, and said if I dug up her charms, the wrong person would buy the house."

He shot another look at Frieda's house. "She sounds dangerous."

"Oh, I don't think so. My friend Vivi—who lives right there," she said, pointing across the street, "says Frieda is eccentric but harmless."

He turned back to Kate. "If she gives you any trouble at all, you let me know. I'll take care of her."

She did not want to be the source of any conflict in this neighborhood, and certainly didn't want to set neighbor against neighbor by idle gossip."Please don't worry about it. She's a bit eccentric, but rather old and frail. And according to Vivi, everyone here likes her. No worries. Truly."

He continued to regard her somberly, but finally nodded. "If you say so. But I'll tell you this. I don't want her messing around in my backyard. If she has something buried back there, I'll dig it up. I plan to have a vegetable garden and flower beds. Will you show me where she was digging?"

Kate glanced at her watch. This impromptu visit was stretching into something she hadn't planned for. "OK. But it'll have to be quick. I need to run an errand in the city."

As they walked toward the backyard, Joe continued his easy repartee. "You work from home, do you?"

"Yes. I'm a crochet designer."

"Interesting. I take it that crochet design is something you like?"

"Oh, yes!" She gave him a big smile. "I love it."

"Do men crochet?"

"Anyone who wants to can crochet," she said with enthusiasm. "Where I'm from, back in Stony Point, Maine, I knew several fellows who crocheted. My agent, Adam Vargas, loves to crochet."

"Maybe you'll teach me sometime."

She thought about his poor eyesight and wasn't sure what to say, but he didn't give her opportunity to reply.

"Pardon me for saying this, but I can't help noticing that you seem a little on edge," he said as they reached the backyard.

"I hit an unexpected bump in the road yesterday, and I'm a little distracted by it. I may have to re-create a lot of work that was lost. Plus, I'm really busy. Starting a new career is exciting, but it does take a lot of time."

"I'm sure it does. I'm sorry you've had problems."

She really did not want to get involved in such a personal conversation with someone she barely knew. "What kind of work do you do, Joe?"

"I used to restore old cars."

"Used to?"

"I sold my shop recently, so I'm retired now. My eyes, you know."

"That must be tough, not having good vision. But there's surgery for cataracts now, relatively quick and painless, I believe." When he did not reply, she moved on, and said, "Do you miss it? Working on cars, I mean?"

"I do, and I'll do it again one of these days, but more as a hobby than a business."

Kate led him to the area and pointed. "Right there is where she buried something. But look!" She went closer. "There's a hole. Someone dug up Frieda's offering."

They stared down at the small hole that measured about a foot deep and a few inches wide. He turned a questioning look to her.

"It wasn't me, I assure you," she said. "She let me know

I wasn't welcome in no uncertain terms."

He scowled. "She had no right to vandalize this property, nor to chase you away from it."

Kate made a dismissive gesture. "I'm sure she meant no harm. And as for the hole that's there now, Vivi says there are a lot of armadillos in the area. Maybe they did it."

He shrugged. "Perhaps. I know nothing about them." He gazed at the hole, then added, "This Vivi. Do you think she might have dug up whatever that woman buried?"

"Goodness no. Not Vivi."

"At any rate, I will be turning this into a garden." He glanced at Kate's backyard. "Yours is rather plain too."

"I moved here in early September and haven't done much to the place." She smiled at him, and held out her hand. "It's been so nice to visit with you, Joe, but I really must get into the city and back home so I can attend to my work."

He clasped her hand warmly and covered it with his other. "Why don't you come in and have some tea first?"

"That sounds lovely, but another time. I really must get going."

She tried to pull her hand free, but he tightened his hold, just a fraction, then smiled and let go.

"I understand. Another time, then."

"You have a lot to do, getting settled."

"I do. At least let me walk you to your car."

As she drove to the yarn shop, Kate thought about the exchange with Joe Vestal. It was apparent that he liked her, and that bothered her for a number of reasons. For one thing, he was married. For another, he was quite a bit older. And lastly, but not of little importance, she was not attracted to him. The only man she might be attracted to would be a tall, handsome Texas detective with a killer smile and dark blue eyes.

I'll just have to make sure Joe understands I am not interested, on any level, she thought as she arrived at Once Upon a Yarn.

Paige was helping a trio of women when Kate entered the store. She glanced up, smiled slightly, but turned her attention immediately back to her customers. Kate poured herself a cup of coffee, then browsed while waiting for Paige to be free. She decided that for her, going into a yarn shop was as bad as a dieter going into a bakery. She wanted one of everything.

She spotted a new blend of thread that looked much more delicate than it was, and the label declared it was "tangle-proof" and "knot-proof."

That would be a first, she thought. If one did not want tangles and knots in the thread, it was best to crochet carefully and keep the tension consistent. Deciding to test the product, she picked up a skein of soft ecru to purchase. If the thread were everything it claimed to be, she would buy more and make a lovely, lacey bolero.

"Hi, Kate," Paige said, approaching. She seemed somewhat frazzled.

"Are you OK?"

Paige gave her a weary smile. "I'm all right, but tired. It's been a busy day."

"I'm sorry you're tired, but a busy day is a good thing, yes?"

"It is, actually." She touched Kate's arm. "You look a little beat yourself."

"I'm a little disheartened, but I'm eager to move forward."

"I like your spirit. Maybe there is something in this envelope that will encourage you."

Kate took the white, sealed business envelope from Paige. On the outside, someone had written "For Kate."

"Thanks," she said, "but I don't think this slipped from my portfolio. I don't recognize it at all." She tore open the envelope and pulled out a single sheet of unlined printer paper.

"Guess who has your sketches?"

Fifteen

"What's wrong?" Paige asked as Kate's hands trembled and her eyes gave the sheet of paper a horrified stare. Kate silently handed the note to her.

"Huh?" Paige lifted her mystified gaze to Kate's, then looked down at the note again. "What do you suppose this means?"

"I have no idea."

Paige shook her head. "I don't either. It's almost as if someone is holding your designs for ransom and simply hasn't made a demand."

Kate felt her heart and stomach plummet.

"Oh my," she said faintly. "Surely not."

Paige fluttered one hand. "No, of course not. I shouldn't have said that. It was just a silly notion that popped into my brain. I think it's far more likely that someone is playing a trick on you."

"A cruel trick. Who did you say gave you this note?"

"A man brought it to the counter. He said it was lying on the floor near the baby yarn, and he thought someone might have dropped it out of a purse or diaper bag."

"Just lying on the floor, huh?"

"That's what he said."

"Who was the guy?"

"I've never seen him before. I doubt if I would recognize him if he walked in here right now. He asked me to help him choose crochet items for his wife as a surprise, and he bought a ton of stuff."

"Did you see anyone in the baby yarn section before him?"

Paige thought about it for a little while. "I believe there was a young couple back there. She was pregnant. But honestly, I've been so busy today that I don't really remember when they were in." She gave Kate an apologetic smile. "I'm so sorry."

She dropped her gaze to the paper in Kate's hand. "But if I were you, I'd take that straight to the police, anyway."

"That's what I intend to do. I'll see you later, Paige. Thanks."

She drove to the Sage Hills Police Department and marched in with the note. A young officer met her at the front desk.

"Help you?" he said.

"This was left for me at the Once Upon a Yarn shop." She handed over the envelope and its message.

"Once Upon a Yarn shop?"

"A yarn store in Fort Worth." Kate took a deep breath and started over. "I was in here yesterday to make a report about someone stealing my professional portfolio. Obviously, the person who wrote this is the thief."

He read the note, then looked at her questioningly as he handed it back. "Do you know who wrote this?"

"I have no idea."

A small frown creased between his eyebrows. "Do you have the envelope?"

She passed it across the desk to him, and he gazed at it as if it held the world's secrets before flipping it over. "No return address." He looked up. "Ma'am, what do you want us to do?"

"Find my portfolio, of course."

"There is nothing here to identify the sender, and besides that, there's really nothing menacing about this note."

"But ..." She sought for the right words. "That portfolio represents years of work. The sketches are protected by copyright."

He merely looked at her.

"There might be fingerprints on this note, right?" she added.

"Could be. But what good are fingerprints when there is no crime?"

"I'm telling you, there *is* a crime. My sketches have been stolen!"

"Basically, all this note says," he said, tapping it with his forefinger, "is 'Guess who?' There's no demand for money and there's no threat of bodily harm."

"Are you telling me you can't you do anything? Nothing at all?"

"I'm sorry, ma'am, but unless someone says 'I stole your sketches' and signs his name, our hands are tied. I'll copy the note and envelope and put it with your original report."

"I see."

"Sorry, ma'am," the officer quietly said again after copying the evidence. "I know you're frustrated, and I don't blame you. But if you get another message, something with a threat, or an acknowledgment of stolen property, let us know."

She nodded, took the note, thanked him, and left.

As she pulled into her driveway a bit later, a splash of scarlet near the front door caught her eye and changed the direction of her concern.

"What in the world? Has Frieda done something to my porch?"

She braked and got out of the van almost before it stopped. She rushed to her tiny porch to see a blood-red rose in full bloom on the bottom step. Kate gaped at it for a moment then shot a look up and down the street, as if the person who left it might be standing around, waiting for her. She saw no one, but grabbed the flower, and ignoring the thorns that pierced her hand, marched down the sidewalk and then up Frieda's walk to the front door.

"Frieda." She pushed the doorbell. When the woman failed to appear, Kate pressed the bell again, then pounded on the door. "*Frieda*!"

The woman's absence from the door didn't fool Kate. Frieda rarely went anywhere beyond the neighborhood. In fact, Kate had seen Murray's Market deliver groceries to her front door.

"I know you're home. All I want to know is the significance of this rose. I don't like people playing tricks on me."

"Kate."

She turned to see Joe striding toward her.

"Kate, what's wrong?"

She took a few steps toward him so she wouldn't have to raise her voice again.

"This!" She held up the rose.

"It's very beautiful."

"I suppose it is, but I'm sure it's some kind of prank or trick or charm from Frieda. I mean, who else would put a rose on someone's doorstep?"

"Maybe a secret admirer?"

She couldn't help but laugh at that. "I hardly think so! And wouldn't a secret admirer leave more than just one? I mean, a dozen roses might say 'I like you,' but only one seems a little stingy."

Joe screwed up his face in thought. "I never thought of it that way. You could be right." He met her eyes. "I've never been the recipient of secret admiration."

"Oh, I bet you have," she said. "You just didn't know it because no one gave you roses." She glanced over her shoulder at Frieda's house. "She's obviously not going to answer the door. And I need to get back to work."

She started walking back to her house and Joe fell into step with her.

"Would you like that cup of tea now?" he asked.

She pondered, not wanting to hurt his feelings, but also not wanting to encourage him.

"Maybe another time, Joe. I really must get to work, but thank you so much for the offer."

An expression shot across his face, quickly there, quickly gone. Kate wasn't sure if she'd seen hurt or irritation. Either way, she felt bad about it.

"We'll have a cuppa another time, OK?"

He smiled. "Sure. You go on back to work now. I have some things to take care of myself."

He stood where he was until she reached her front door, as if he were watching out for her safety. It touched her that he cared enough to do that. She smiled at him, unlocked the door, and went inside.

She had no more than settled at her table when her phone rang.

"It's Adam. How are things going?"

"Hi, Adam. Things are a little odd. Someone left a weird note for me at Paige's shop today, and when I got home, I found that someone had left a rose on my doorstep."

"That's a little peculiar, isn't it? Tell me about the note."

She told him about it and added, "All Paige knows is that someone found it on the floor in her shop and turned it in."

"Do you think the same person left the rose on your doorstep?"

"I don't know. From what Vivi has told me about Frieda Mahl, the woman uses flowers and other plants a lot in her 'magic,' so I suspect she might have left it here as some kind of spell to turn me into a frog or whatever. It's apparent she doesn't like me, but Vivi says she's harmless."

"Do you think she wrote the note?" he asked.

"She could have, but I doubt she did. She never leaves the neighborhood. Besides, why wouldn't she just leave the note on my doorstep with the rose, or put it in my mailbox?"

"Good point."

"I took the note to the police station, but there's nothing they can do." She huffed. "It's all a jumbled-up mini-mystery."

"I'm sorry to hear all this, and I understand how you feel. But neither the note nor the rose seem to present any kind of threat or danger. In fact, they seem to be gestures made to annoy or frighten you more than anything else." He paused for a moment as if letting the words sink in. "Can you put them out of your mind?"

She took a deep breath. "I can certainly try, because believe me, this is no fun."

"I know," he said, "but I have some news that might help."

"Oh?" In spite of everything, she felt a bright stirring of interest. "What is it?"

"I've been in touch with Alexus Lauren, your editor at Brighton & Craig. I've told her what happened to your portfolio, and she's going to set up a meeting between you and a technical editor. If you can re-sketch as many designs as possible between now and Thursday morning, Alexus and I believe that with Robin helping you, we can get everything back on track. What do you think?"

The news shot through her like a rush of pure sugar.

"I think that's the best news I've heard in a while! If I get right on it, I believe I can re-sketch the designs, but I don't want to rush making the pattern. Doing so might cause me to make an error, and I don't want to do that."

"Of course you don't. And neither do the rest of us. Robin is quite young, but she is experienced, and she's very good at what she does. Would you be up for a meeting with her on Thursday?"

"Absolutely! Anything to rebuild my portfolio."

As soon as she was off the phone, Kate picked up her sketchpad and got to work, sketching with renewed spirit and vigor. She drew the favorite design of those she had lost, the beautifully delicate evening gown. She remembered how much Paige had loved it.

After a couple of hours, her back felt hard as a brick and she had a raging headache at the base of her skull. Kate recognized these symptoms. She had been sitting in one place for too long, and the tension of the last two days had gripped her even harder. A brisk walk usually helped to limber up tight muscles, so she put away her sketchpad and went outside.

The area around Hawkins Drive was pleasant and well kept, filled with neat, modest houses and lawns. She enjoyed looking at the neighborhood, but as daylight began to fade, she hurried back home. She glanced across the street at Vivi's house, wishing her friend were there instead of working that huge convention.

"I hope she's doing OK," Kate murmured to herself.

Kate went through the ritual of locking all the doors and windows and then double-checking them. She made sure her blinds were firmly drawn before fixing herself a sandwich and glass of milk. In the bathroom, she turned on the warm water and sprinkled lavender-scented bath salts. It was going to feel good to slide down into that fragrant warmth and soak. Who would believe her if she told them sketching and designing patterns could make one so tired?

As the water ran, she went into the bedroom to get fresh nightclothes from the dresser drawer. Her mind spun with the joyous anticipation of meeting Alexus and Robin on Thursday. She couldn't wait to share her ideas and hear what the editors had to say.

Kate burned with an urge to start crocheting the evening dress with the fitted bodice. The image shone so brightly in her mind, she knew it was destined to be her next project. She hoped the editors at Brighton & Craig agreed.

I'll sketch some more tonight, and if I get everything completed tomorrow, I might just start crocheting the evening gown as early as tomorrow night, she thought as she turned to pluck her robe off the foot of the bed. *That way—*

The thought died the moment her glance landed on the blood-red rose lying on her pillow.

Sixteen

Kate gaped at the rose, not fully comprehending what she saw. Then, as her wits gathered to form thoughts, the clothes fell from her trembling hands, and she grabbed hold of the wall to keep from falling.

Who was in here? And when? What does this mean?

Kate felt frozen to the very marrow of her bones, but finally was able to shake herself into action. She grabbed up her baseball bat and got her cellphone to call Peter.

"Someone has been in my house!" she nearly shrieked the moment he answered.

"What? Are you hurt? Are you all right?"

"I'm OK, but there's a rose on my pillow."

"A rose on your pillow? When was it put there?"

"I was here until about thirty minutes ago, when I took a walk."

"And when you came home, you found a rose on your pillow?"

"Yes." A new thought occurred. "Peter. You didn't ... did you? That is, leave me a rose at the door earlier and ...?"

There was the briefest silence. "No, Kate. Absolutely not. For one thing, I'd never break into your house. For another, when I give you roses, I will hand them to you myself. Now, give me the details of this. You said someone left a rose at your door *and* on your pillow?"

"Yes. When I came home, there it was. But this other one in my bedroom wasn't here. Getting into my house takes it to a whole different level than just leaving it on my porch. Peter ..." Her voice caught, and she cleared her throat. "I'm really scared."

"I understand. Listen, I'm on my way right now. You sit tight, and don't open the door for anyone but me. OK?"

"Yes. Yes, thank you."

Darkness had fallen fully by that time. She paced the floor while waiting for Peter to arrive, jumping at every sound. Who had left those roses? Some unknown person? Frieda? Joe? Adam, or maybe Paige? What about Nick? Had he somehow found her? Kate hated these suspicious notions crashing around in her mind. Granted, she did not know any of these people very well, but with the exception of Frieda and Nick, she felt each one was her friend.

It seemed like hours until Peter arrived, but it was really only minutes. She was so glad to open the door and see his six-foot-plus frame in her doorway, she all but hurled herself into his arms.

"Aw, now, Kate," he said kindly, holding her. "It's all right. You're safe."

She choked back her tears, determined not to make a scene.

"Thank you," she managed to squeak out.

She wasn't sure how long she stood in the protective circle of Peter's arms, but he released her and said, "May we go inside?"

"We?" Kate wiped the heels of her hands across her eyes. A bleary-eyed glance beyond Peter showed two uniformed officers from Sage Hills and flashing lights turning the night red and blue.

"Of course," she said, stepping back. As she watched the men enter, their strong bodies, shining badges, holstered pistols, and efficiency of purpose seemed to fill her small home. Their gazes scoured everything, as if nothing too small could escape notice.

Certainly different from the last time the police were here, she thought, grateful that the tired, older officer was not with them.

"I called the Sage Hills P.D. to investigate," Peter said. "I have no jurisdiction here."

"I understand."

"OK if we look around, ma'am?" an officer asked.

"Yes, please. Anything you need to do." She clamped her mouth shut.

"So, Kate," Peter said, steering her toward the love seat, "tell me again what happened." One of the Sage Hill officers stood nearby with a notebook and pen.

She sat down and related everything that had happened.

"You said you locked your doors before you left?" the local policeman asked.

"Yes! Absolutely. After everything that has happened since I moved to Texas, I keep my doors and windows locked." She looked at Peter. "I'm thinking of getting a dog. A big one."

Peter hadn't taken his eyes off her. He smiled gently and took one of her cold hands in his large warm one. "Maybe you should get some motion lights or a home security system."

"I'll think about it," she said, but she knew the cost of installation and monthly fees would be beyond her ability right then. "Maybe I should get a pistol."

"Can you shoot?" Peter asked, one eyebrow raised.

"I don't know a thing about guns," she admitted, "and I don't like the idea of having one around. But right now, I'm willing to learn."

"I could teach you. Now, show me where you found the rose."

One of the Sage Hills policemen went outside as Peter and the other officer followed her down the short hallway to her bedroom. She pointed to the rose still lying on the plump white pillow with its eyelet-trimmed case.

"I came out of the bathroom to get my clothes, and there it was." Both men noted the rose, then studied the room. Kate's glance fell to her pajamas and underwear on the floor where she'd dropped them. Her face flamed, but she figured grabbing the garments and trying to hide them would bring more attention to them. Instead she did her best to ignore their presence.

"Look around carefully," Peter said. "Is anything missing—anything out of place?"

Kate liked to keep her bedroom neat and spare, with everything put away. She ran a glance around the room.

"Nothing," she said.

The Sage Hills officer plucked the rose off the pillow with his gloved hand and slid it into a bag he took from his pocket.

"Let's go back to the living room and sit down." Peter gently took her arm to escort her. Feeling jumpy and discombobulated, she settled down on the love seat while Peter wrote a few notes in a little notebook he took from his pocket.

The second local officer came in.

"You find anything, Johnny?" Peter asked him.

"I talked to the neighbors, but none of them have seen anything suspicious." He turned his attention to Kate. "The fellow next door said to tell you he'd be happy to camp out here in your living room for the night, if you'd like him to."

Peter's eyes narrowed. "I thought the house next door was empty."

"That's Joe. He just moved in."

"So you don't know him."

"No, but he's very nice."

"If you don't know him, how do you know he's very nice?"

"Because he is. Would an un-nice person offer to stay here?"

"Yes."

She crimped her lips and cast about for a good response. Was Peter's heightened concern balanced by a bit of jealousy? Surely not! Surely he was acting purely as a law enforcement officer.

Hoping to mollify him, she said, "I'm touched by Joe's offer and by your concern, Peter, but you should know that Joe is older. Quite a bit older, in fact. He's nearly blind, and he doesn't hear very well. I doubt the man could do much if someone tried to break in."

"That's right," Johnny said.

"I see. What about the woman a couple of doors down? Did you talk to her?" he asked the other officer.

"No one came to the door, and no lights on."

"She probably won't come to the door, either," Kate said. "She's odd."

"Odd enough to get into your house and leave a rose?"

"Maybe. If anyone would do something like that, Frieda would be my first guess. When I found the rose on my doorstep, I went straight to her house, but she never came to the door. I'm pretty sure she was home, because she never goes anywhere."

"Better follow up with her then," Peter said, looking at Officer Johnny. Kate knew he couldn't give orders to the local police since he was on the Fort Worth police force, but she saw plainly that the officers respected him enough to listen to what he had to say.

"I'll do it," Johnny said. He looked at the other officer. "You want to get the kit, Haynes?"

The policeman nodded and went outside.

Kate got up and took the envelope with the anonymous note from her purse.

She handed it to Peter. "Someone found this at Once Upon a Yarn today and turned it in to Paige."

He took it from her and read it. He frowned, turned the page over as if looking for more writing, then examined the envelope. "You recognize this handwriting?"

"No."

"Did Paige say who found it?"

"A customer who was buying some yarn for his wife. She said he found it on the floor."

Peter slid the note back into the envelope. "Have you received any more notes like this?"

"No. Just the one." She glanced at Johnny. "I showed it to an officer at the Sage Hills police station, but he didn't seem to think it was anything. He did make a copy of it to file with my original report, but that was all."

"He's probably right," Peter said, "but if you don't mind, I'll take this with me. I'll file it with the report I made, just in case the theft of your portfolio occurred in Fort Worth."

She nodded. "Please do."

He and Johnny exchanged glances but said nothing. Kate knew the silent communication between them was a reassurance that Johnny would be alert and aware of the situation. She was grateful the man worked for the Sage Hills P.D.

The officer who had gone outside returned with a fingerprint kit.

"Let me get your prints for comparison," he said to Kate.

"Can you stay with Vivi tonight?" Peter asked while the other man recorded her prints.

"No. She's super-involved with a really important convention right now, and she said she might have to stay overnight at the hotel."

He tapped his forefinger against his lips, eyes narrowed. "What about your agent?"

"Adam? What about him?"

"Can he take you in for a—"

She shook her head vigorously. "He's my agent, not my keeper. Besides, I'll be all right. I keep the phone right beside me everywhere I go. I'm a light sleeper, so I'll hear any little noise. Besides, I have my baseball bat, in case I need to slug someone."

Peter smiled at her words, then turned to Johnny. "Will you see to it that patrols are increased through here?"

"I'll do it," he said, and gave Kate a reassuring smile.

"Kate." Peter took one hand in both of his and looked in her eyes. "Listen to me. I know you're frightened, and that's understandable. Whoever left the rose on your doorstep and in your room did it while you were gone. I doubt he'll try anything when you're here. Keep your doors and windows locked. Be wary when you come home, but try not to worry too much. Believe me, you're in good hands." He squeezed her fingers and gave her a smile. "I'll do everything I can to help you. Trust me. OK?"

His words made her feel safe and warm, and that was something she needed to feel right then. She returned his smile.

"OK," she said. "I'll try my best."

Later, as wind prowled through the night and the moon created shadows outside her house, Kate burrowed further into her bed and prayed Peter would be able to keep his word.

Seventeen

Wednesday morning, Kate rose well before sunup. She showered and dressed, then worked with single-minded intent, purposely allowing no thought in her head except the designs that came from her pencil to her sketchpad.

The day was still young when her doorbell rang. She grabbed the baseball bat and peeked through the peephole. She leaned the bat against the wall and opened the door.

"Good morning, Joe."

She was glad she understood that his hard stare was Joe's way of trying to see her more clearly. Otherwise, she might have thought he was looking for secrets locked in her soul.

"Good morning. I want to tell you that I didn't sleep a wink last night," he said.

"I'm sorry to hear that! Are you ill?"

"No. But honestly, Kate, I am worried about you." He clenched and unclenched his jaw. If he hadn't told her that he was worried, Kate would have read his tension as anger. "I saw the police show up here last night, lights blazing. One came to my house and questioned me."

She stepped onto the porch. "I'm so sorry, but—"

He held up one hand and shook his head. "Don't be sorry. They're doing their job. The officer talked to me for a while, you know, asking who I was, how long I'd been here, and if I knew you. Then he asked if I had seen anyone prowling around the neighborhood. I told him about that weirdo next door to me, of course. Tell me the truth: Is she—or someone else—causing you trouble?"

His concern touched her. Here was a kindly, handicapped, older man, and his concern was for her. Even if she were to tell him all about the strange things that had happened to her in the last few weeks, there was nothing he could do about any of it, except worry more. He had enough on his plate.

"I kept my eye on your place all night," he added.

"Oh, no! You didn't, did you? I'm so sorry—"

"Stop apologizing. It's not your fault. A patrol car passed through the neighborhood every so often, and I felt pretty confident you were safe. But I needed to make sure."

She felt both comforted and distressed. "I wish you wouldn't worry about me, Joe. I'm fine. Truly I am."

He crossed his arms over his chest and never dropped his gaze. "Now, why don't I believe you?"

She offered him the best smile she could muster, one that she hoped looked full of confidence. "Probably because I usually come across as a bit timid and fearful. I used to be that way, but I'm not like that any longer. I refuse to let anyone or anything keep me down."

"Let's assume someone actually gets into your house and lies in wait for you, or enters while you are there—God forbid. How do plan to protect yourself?"

"Why, I will knock his block off! I bought a Louisville Slugger, and I'm keeping it close to me all the time."

"I see. What about a gun?"

"I don't have one yet, but Peter said he'd show me how to use a pistol."

He turned his head slightly. "How's that?"

"I said I don't have a gun, but if I get one, Peter will teach me to shoot it."

"Peter?"

"Peter Matthews. My … um, my friend. He's a detective with the Fort Worth police."

Joe said nothing for a long time. When he finally looked away, he rubbed the back of his neck.

"Well, maybe I've underestimated you." He brought his gaze back to her, and softened it with a smile. "I guess you're stronger than you look."

She flexed her arms. "I'm a real she-girl."

"I'm convinced."

"Good. Now you can stop worrying."

"But I'm going to keep an eye on you, because that's the kind of neighbor I am. I don't want to see anyone get hurt."

"Thank you. And please do me a favor. Tonight, I want you to get some sleep." She made a move to go back into the house, but he continued to stand expectantly. "Is there something else?"

"After the night you had, I'd like to take you to breakfast this morning."

Her face broke into a warm smile. "Thank you, Joe. That is so sweet, and I'd love to, but I can't. I have an appointment in the city tomorrow, and I need to have everything ready for them."

His expression did not change, but he nodded. "Oh, well. That does have priority over me, doesn't it?"

"Maybe another time."

He turned his head slightly. "How's that?"

"We'll have breakfast another time?" she said loudly.

"Oh." He nodded as he moved away. "All right. And you look mighty pretty in that blue dress. You should wear blue more often."

"Thanks, Joe. For the invitation and the compliment."

He walked away as she spoke, and raised one hand in farewell, but never glanced back at her.

Thursday morning as she prepared for the meeting with Alexus, Kate found her mind creeping back into a place of unease. As Peter had assured her, no intruder had tried to enter her home while she was there. But what might she find when she came home?

I refuse to think about that now, she thought. Her focus needed to be completely on the upcoming meeting. She dressed in a light gray sheath dress with a mid-length crocheted black jacket and simple black pumps. She felt the outfit symbolized the elegant yet simple lines of her designs. A final sharp perusal of her appearance in the full-length mirror on her bedroom closet door satisfied Kate that she looked all right. With nervous excitement running through every cell in her body, she picked up her purse, made sure she had her keys and cellphone, and grabbed up the bat so she'd have it with her when she returned. She locked her doors and headed for Fort Worth.

She arrived at Brighton & Craig Publishing ten minutes early. Kate liked to arrive early for appointments; it gave her time to take a few relaxing breaths and gather her thoughts. It also gave her a moment to convert her natural shyness into something akin to quiet confidence. Even so, she was glad to see Adam's white Prius in the parking lot.

The building that housed the publishing company was not as large as Kate had expected. A steel-and-glass box with shining windows, it stood a mere two stories tall, and she could see light reflecting from white tile floors before she opened the wide door. Holding a folder with her redrawn designs, she stood a couple of steps inside the door, looking around.

Given how open the place appeared from the outside, the reception area was rather small and cozy. It had a cherrywood desk with a couple of bronze-colored leather chairs flanking a small table. Two hallways led farther into the building on either side of the desk. The sage-green interior wall boasted covers of Brighton & Craig books in sleek white frames.

No one sat behind the desk to greet visitors, so Kate took the opportunity to examine the book covers. Colorful, with clear, sharp images and with author names and titles in simple fonts, the books gave the impression of quality and class. Kate was more excited than she could say to know that one day soon, her own designs would reside between the hard covers of beautiful books.

"Good mornin'!"

Kate turned to see a fair-skinned girl with dark hair that hung in thick curls nearly to her tiny waist.

"I'm Jennifer Joy, and you must be Kate Stevens!" She approached on ridiculously tall stilettoes without staggering a single step. The top of her head barely reached Kate's chin. Surely this child couldn't be more than twelve, if that. What were her parents thinking, allowing her to wear those shoes and have a job?

She smiled, showing lovely white teeth. Kate noted there was not a single freckle on that milky white skin.

"It's such an honor to meet you," Jennifer Joy said. "I've admired your work for a long time." Her voice dripped Texas honey in such an endearing way that Kate was enchanted.

I wonder what a 'long time' is, in Jennifer Joy years, Kate thought, laughing inside.

"I do hope you design outfits for children. My daughter is so girly that I know she'd look cuter than a bug in a lacy, crocheted dress."

"Your daughter?"

"Uh-hmm," she said, nodding and smiling. "Come this way, and I'll take you to Robin's office. Adam is already here."

As Kate followed the girl down the hallway, she said, "How old is your daughter?"

"She'll be ten next month."

Kate was so shocked that she nearly walked into the wall.

"Here you go!" Jennifer Joy sang out as she swept one hand toward an open door on the right. "Miss Kate is here, y'all," she said.

Kate walked into a small, spartan office with bare, wheat-colored walls. A desk and two small chairs overfilled the space. Adam and the young auburn-haired woman behind the desk held crochet hooks and worked almost in sync with pale gray yarn. They stopped as Kate entered. Adam got to his feet to greet her with a quick kiss on the cheek.

"Hello, Kate," he said with a big smile. "Kate, this is Robin Gray."

Robin was thin and attractive, extremely neat with a boyish haircut and tailored azure-blue suit.

"How do you do," Kate said, thankful her voice came out confident and strong.

Robin laid her hook and yarn on her desktop and rose to shake Kate's hand. "It's good to meet you," she said. "Please have a seat." Her gaze traveled appreciatively over Kate's jacket.

Adam sat down and resumed crocheting. As Kate settled in the other chair, she eyed Adam's project. From the width and bulk of it, Kate knew he was making a throw.

"Lovely," she said, touching a soft edge.

"New yarn Robin wants to test-drive, so I am." He held up what he'd finished so far. "It's bulky and soft and works up quickly, but it also has a tendency to twist as it comes out of the skein."

Kate winced. Yarn that twisted could indicate poor quality control.

Robin had returned to the chair behind her desk, and her gaze was now focused unblinkingly on Kate. It seemed to Kate that the young woman perched on the edge of the chair like an alert bird. Her spine could not possibly be straighter.

"Adam has told me of your recent problems. I'm so sorry to hear about them."

Kate nodded and plucked absently at the edge of the folder holding her sketches.

"I've been beside myself worrying about the lost designs, especially if someone were to claim them as their own instead of mine," she said. "I didn't know what to do except to try to re-create them." She held up the folder. "I think I did all right, but I'm afraid you might not find them as inspiring as the original sketches."

"I have seen your original designs, Kate," Adam said. "I can vouch for you if it ever comes to that. For that matter, so can Paige Bryant."

She gave him a grateful smile. "Thank you."

With her clasped hands resting as if made of marble on the desktop, Robin's gaze never left Kate's face. It was as though she tried to probe the inner workings of Kate's mind. Then she smiled, and her face was transformed into something warm and beautiful and personable, and Kate instantly felt better.

"Worry and fear can be such burdens, can't they?" Robin leaned forward. "I'd like to take some of that burden off your shoulders."

Adam beamed at both women. “See? I told you Robin would save the day.”

The woman sat even straighter. “Thank you, Adam.”

“She takes her work very seriously,” he said in a mock undertone.

“Is she here?” a rich, throaty voice called down the hallway. A moment later, a lovely and curvaceous African-American woman entered the room. Her smile seemed to come from her very soul, and the aura she exuded was one of nurture and industry.

“You must be Kate,” she said before anyone else had a chance to make introductions. “I’m Alexus Lauren, your editor.” She glanced at Adam. “No, no, you stay sitting right there, Adam. I can make myself at home on the corner of this desk.”

She leaned her hips against it, resting both palms on the desktop.

“We were just talking about the theft of Kate’s portfolio,” Robin said.

Alexus’s smile slipped from her face and she shook her head.

“I don’t understand why people do some of the things they do. I bet you have been worried sick, haven’t you?”

“Oh yes I have,” Kate said, meaning it from the bottom of her heart.

Alexus leaned forward and laid one soft warm hand over Kate’s. “One thing that you need to remember is that we already have your designs, patterns and text for the first book. So we won’t be held up in getting that book produced.”

“That’s a comfort,” Kate said. “But I keep telling myself that re-creating the sketches will take time I could have used for making the patterns.”

"Adam Vargas, what a worrier you've brought to me!" Alexus laughed.

"Being a worrier isn't altogether a bad thing," Robin said. "It means you're committed to getting your work done, and doing it right."

"I never thought about it quite like that," Kate said, smiling.

"But who needs the headaches that worry brings?" Alexus said. She shifted her gaze to Kate's bundle. "What's in your folder? Something for us, I hope?"

"These are some of the lost sketches I've re-created."

"Bless your heart!" Alexus said, holding out one hand. Kate passed the folder to her and watched as the woman opened it. Robin stood and leaned forward to look at the sketches over Alexus's shoulder.

"Oh my!" she said as Alexus passed the first one to her. "How beautiful."

"Robin, would you look at this one? Gorgeous!" Alexus said.

For a few tense moments, neither woman said a word as they looked at the designs. Kate sent a big-eyed glance to Adam, who gave her a beatific smile and never paused in his crochet.

"They love them," he said with great assurance.

"Indeed we do!" Alexus murmured.

"If these are second-best to what you did originally, then those originals must have been out of this world," Robin said, looking up.

After a while, Alexus pushed out a deep, satisfied breath and slid all the sketches but one back into the folder.

"I want this dress included in the first book. It's going to be on the cover, if I have my way." She said this as casually as if she'd mentioned she wanted Kate to crochet her a dishcloth. She held up the sketch of the evening dress.

Kate blinked, feeling her heart bound, then sink. "But I haven't made it yet. I haven't even started!"

"Then you better get busy," Alexus said, smiling but serious. "This is a signature piece. A showstopper, in fact. We must lead with it."

"Yes," Kate said faintly. "OK."

"I'll amend the contract, and we'll initial it. And then, Kate Stevens," she said, looking straight into Kate's eyes, "work up a proposal for book number two. In fact, work up proposals for books three, four, and five. Then get that evening dress made." She shifted her gaze to Adam. "We are going to go places with this young woman."

"I told you so," Adam said, his glance going from one face to the other. Kate wasn't sure if his words were for her or for Alexus and Robin, but at that moment she was so full of elation and amazement, it didn't matter.

Jennifer Joy popped into the doorway of the office and drawled, "Y'all! I want her to design a line of clothes for young girls."

Alexus beamed. "Of course she will. You see, Kate, you are going to be popular, and your work is going to be in demand." She pushed away from the desk. "Robin will tell you what she's going to be doing for you." They shook hands once again. "It was such a pleasure and honor to meet you. Adam, stop by my office before you leave. Jennifer Joy, please get me a coffee? See y'all later," she said as she walked out of the office.

Kate blinked. The woman, for all her motherly charm and calm nature, was a force to be reckoned with.

"I will be checking all your patterns for accuracy and skill level." Robin said. "I will also crochet the garments to see if they live up to our expectations."

Robin's clipped words brought Kate back to earth with

an unceremonious thump. For a moment, Kate felt affronted and offended. Her mouth wagged a few times.

"I was very careful when I made the patterns," Kate finally said, "and I've marked the skill level on each one."

Adam reached over and patted her hand as though to remind her all was well.

"I'm sure you have," Robin said crisply, "but it's my job to double-check everything, Kate. I do it for every pattern we publish. We mustn't let a missed stitch or wrong row count slip past us." She offered a reassuring smile. "Please don't take it personally."

"It's her job," Adam echoed.

Kate felt a little foolish and petty, but not too much. The designs were hers, and she would never approach any of the work she did carelessly.

"All right," she said, feeling better. "But I do try to be as meticulous with my notes and sketches as possible."

"Of course you do. I'm sure of it," Robin said. "If you have any designs from your first book already made, I'd like to see them right away. We're going to need photographs."

"Uh-oh."

"Uh-oh?"

"Most of those garments have been sold." She looked at Adam. "In Paige's shop."

"Well, then," Robin said briskly, "we'll just bring in some of our techs to crochet them for us. We have some skilled needlecrafters."

"All right."

They talked for a while longer, Robin laying out a timeline, with definite goals and deadlines. Although the approach seemed almost overwhelming, Kate knew this was the best way to get the work accomplished. She found comfort in that. The last thing Robin did before Kate left her office was to make copies of all the sketches and notes.

"From now on," she said as she handed the folder back to Kate, "back up everything you do on the computer, and make multiple copies of everything. We can't risk another loss."

Feeling a bit stunned by the events of the last hour, but renewed in body, mind, and spirit, Kate left the publishing house. From this point on, she could not allow anyone or anything to distract her from her vision and her career. She must double her efforts to make sure nothing got in her way.

But on the way home, the niggling fear of intruders in her home resurfaced.

I won't let fear of the unknown stop me either, she declared inside her head.

She pulled slowly into her driveway and stopped halfway to the carport, her gaze probing every inch of the house and grounds. Nothing seemed different or out of place; no skulking person peeked at her around any corner. She stared hard at the windows, but did not see so much as a twitch of the curtains.

With bat in hand, she entered the house as if stepping on shards of glass with bare feet. She inspected every room, bat upraised, body so tense she felt she might pull a muscle. By the time Kate was satisfied no one lurked in her home, her arms and legs were trembling like broken tree limbs in winter wind.

To calm herself, she sat down and worked for a couple of hours on the evening gown. The silvery-gray thread worked into a beautiful beginning.

"I'm going to love this!" she said, smiling at the rows she'd just stitched.

She put aside the project to plug in the teapot. She wanted

to brew some Earl Grey tea, and since she had a lot of work to do, she planned to make it strong.

While waiting for the water to boil, Kate fixed a sandwich and checked her email. She smiled to see she had a message from Beverly.

Finally! she thought. *I hope she hasn't been sick.*

She opened the email and read it. Beverly's message was chatty, telling Kate that she had been traveling, staying where there was no WiFi for the Internet, but that she was, at last, settled back at home.

"How are you?" she had written. *"Good things happening in your life? How's the crochet work coming along? Have you been able to keep it going? Well, I must get busy. There's a church social tonight, and I'm supposed to bring cream puffs. Hope I don't eat them all before I have a chance to get them there. LOL."*

While the tea brewed, Kate typed her reply. *"So lovely to hear from you again. I'm glad you had a good time on your travels and are safely back home. Did you work on the baby afghan while you were gone? I'm very busy, especially since someone stole my lovely leather design portfolio and all my sketches. However, I dedicated myself to re-creating what was lost, and am about to start working like mad to crochet an evening dress that will be on the cover of my first book. And now, I must get busy. Take care of yourself, and keep in touch. Don't eat too many cream puffs. Remember your diabetes."*

She sent short replies to emails from friends in Stony Point, looked at a couple of her favorite crochet websites, then closed her browser and shut down her laptop. It was far too easy to be pulled in by the lure of the online world and let hours slip by unnoticed. She now had concrete goals and expectations to meet and would be even more diligent with her time management.

She made good progress on the evening dress, choosing to do the fitted bodice.

If I add a few small Swarovski crystals, she thought as she eyed the lacy mesh, *the end result will be spectacular.* The more she contemplated the idea, the better she liked it, and she fell asleep that night with the image in her mind.

Arising before seven o'clock Friday morning, Kate was eager to work on the dress. As she was buttering her toast, the doorbell rang.

The sky was still pale with wakening. Kate wiped the toast crumbs from her hands on a paper towel, slipped to the front window, and peeked out through the peephole.

"Again?" she whispered.

She ran her hands over her sleep-mussed hair and made sure her robe was neatly tied and then opened her door.

"Good morning, Joe. My, you're up early! I hope you slept well last night."

"I did. How about you?"

"Yes, I did too. And I'm ready and raring to get to work this morning."

"Since you had that appointment yesterday, I want to take you to breakfast today," he said. "There's a good place over on Plains Avenue."

Kate thought about it for a minute. An image of a hearty Texas breakfast, complete with biscuits, gravy, hash browns, and bacon popped into her head. She'd existed on sandwiches and cereal almost exclusively in the last few weeks, and the mere thought of a huge breakfast nearly broke her resolve to work with single-minded intent that day. The vision of the unfinished dress replaced the image of food.

"That sounds so good," she said.

He grinned.

"And I hate to say no," she continued. His grin faded.

"Then say yes."

"I wish I could, Joe, but honestly, I must keep my nose to the grindstone here. The editor at Brighton & Craig—the company that is going to publish my work—wants me to finish several garments for her as soon as possible, so they can photograph them. Not only that, with a spring fashion show I have agreed to do with Paige at Once Upon a Yarn, there is not a moment to waste." She offered him an apologetic smile. "I do hope you understand."

There was a considerable pause. He chewed on a corner of his upper lip while looking at nothing. He rubbed the back of his neck, then looked at her, eyes narrowed.

"Well, Kate, I've tried to be your friend. I moved in next to you, and I've been looking out for you like a big brother. But you keep turning down my overtures of friendship for one reason or another. I hope you don't think I'm trying to pick you up for prurient purposes. I'm a happily married man, and my interest is purely one of being a good neighbor."

His words struck her tender heart. It wasn't her intention to slight or offend anyone, and he had been very kind to her, but she had to keep focused if she wanted to meet deadlines.

"Of course I understand that. You've been a wonderful neighbor. Please don't feel bad because I keep putting you off. It has nothing to do with you. It's just that I have so much to do." He said nothing, and she continued, "I tell you what. Let me see how much I can get done by Sunday. If I've made good progress, maybe we can have Sunday brunch together. Would that work for you?"

He remained silent. His gaze seemed riveted on something beyond her, something only he could see. She recognized that expression. It was the face of someone whose tender feelings had been wounded. Guilt charged sharply through her, but she pushed it back. In this instance, she had to be strong and put herself first.

"All right," he said gruffly. "Sunday brunch."

Kate realized then that no matter how busy she was, if she wanted to keep the goodwill of this new and seemingly lonely neighbor, she needed to carve out a couple of hours to spend with him. She hoped the renovations he was doing on his house would soon be finished so his wife would be there to allay his loneliness. Never having seen his son, she wondered if the young man spent much time with his father. Joe rarely spoke of him.

"Perhaps your son will join us? I haven't met him yet, you know."

"I'm not sure if he will or not. Like you, he stays busy."

She started to speak, but words died on her lips as she caught sight of Frieda Mahl scurrying along the sidewalk, clutching something to her chest, head bent as if facing a strong wind. As soon as she got to Kate's property line she began to scatter bits of something, throwing it like she was broadcasting seed.

"What in the world ...?" Kate mused aloud.

Joe turned, and they both watched the woman as she continued her behavior until she reached the other side of Kate's lot, where she pivoted abruptly and threw bits with the other hand. She started to come up Kate's walkway, muttering and scattering.

"What on earth are you doing, Frieda?" Kate called out.

The woman looked up. When she saw them both, her thin face blanched. She tossed the remainder of what looked like green confetti in their direction, then scurried toward her own house, cutting across all three front lawns.

"Hey!" Joe hollered. "Come back here." He started to take off after her, but Kate restrained him.

"Don't frighten her, please. She's just an eccentric old woman." She went down her walkway and stooped to pick up some of what Frieda had tossed. "It's some kind of dried plant." She sniffed it. "Sage. White sage. She was throwing dried sage in my yard."

"And at you."

"Isn't sage what people burn or sprinkle or something to keep away evil spirits? I guess Frieda thinks I'm evil."

"Who knows what's in her mind? She's obviously disturbed."

Kate nodded as she and Joe watched Frieda dart into her house. Her door slammed like the sound of doom.

"Goodness!" she said.

Joe met her eyes. "You should call the police."

"Oh no. There's no need. She's harmless."

"It's the ones who appear the most harmless that you need to fear."

"Maybe so. But not Frieda. She's lived here a long time, and if she'd been inclined to cause real problems, she would have done so already."

"And how do you know she hasn't?"

"Why, Vivi said she's a bit strange, but the people in the neighborhood like her well enough."

"And Vivi would know?"

"Sure she would. She's lived here quite a while."

"If you want my advice, I wouldn't embrace the veracity of that. I'll bet that woman there," he said, cutting his eyes toward Frieda's house, "has a disturbing past."

A creepy feeling went down Kate's spine, but she wasn't about to let Joe see how his words had affected her.

"I better get back to work," she said, smiling brightly. "Sunday brunch, you and me, for sure."

"Yes. Unless you find something else you'd rather do." He turned as he spoke and started walking, adding over his shoulder, "You best get busy now; you have a lot to do. Take care of yourself, Kate."

"You too. Thanks for everything, Joe."

He said nothing. Thinking he had not heard her, she called out her thanks again, but he kept walking. She watched him go back to his house, and couldn't help the pang of guilt. With his wife still not arrived, and his son too busy to be around a lot … She sighed. The world could be a lonely place.

As the day progressed, Joe's house emitted sounds of hammering and sawing. Kate felt comforted, knowing his work was keeping him occupied, and when he had finished, his wife would join him. She just hoped his eyesight wasn't so bad that he injured himself.

Eighteen

Kate shoved out of her mind every concern she had except getting the evening dress finished. She got up early, stayed up late, ate quick meals, and took quick showers.

Saturday morning, she pinned the back panels of the dress on her dress form and eyed it. The slight train with its delicate crocheted magnolias was lovely but it needed something. Too often, it seemed to Kate, the art of crochet was seen as unwieldy and unnecessary, shoved into a category of Granny's basket of goodies. One of Kate's goals was to bring crochet to a new level in the eyes of potential clients and customers.

The crystals, she thought. *Just a few, scattered throughout like dewdrops on petals.*

The more she thought about it, the more she wondered if crystals were her best choice. Would using them be overdoing the design? She wanted elegance, style, and class, nothing garish or overworked.

With her current budget, she hesitated to invest in expensive crystals and then not use them.

If I placed sequins where crystals might go, I'd get an idea if there would be too much sparkle and shine.

Kate rummaged through her craft supplies, but found no sequins. Nor had she expected to. The only sequins she'd ever had were ones she'd bought for Vanessa years ago to use in her art projects for school. She could have found them at Once Upon a Yarn, but it was in Fort Worth, and she didn't want to waste precious time driving into the city. She opened her laptop to do a search for a nearby crafts or party supply store, and found that Sage Hills had two shops that might carry them.

A little icon flashed, telling her she had unread email messages. Of course she did; she hadn't looked at her email since Wednesday. She opened her account and saw a message from her friend back in Maine, Mary Beth Brock; two from Beverly; and notifications from the crochet and crafting blogs she subscribed to. The blog posts could wait to be read, but she did want to read messages from her friends.

She fixed a glass of iced tea, then sat before her computer to enjoy the next few minutes.

Mary Beth's email was fairly long and chatty, full of witty observations about her days at A Stitch in Time. Kate laughed out loud at the account of Stella Brickson, who was the oldest member of the Hook and Needle Club, and Alice MacFarlane, the free spirit of the group, talking about tattoos.

Kate wrote a quick reply to Mary Beth, ending it with an apology for the brevity of her response. "I'll call you later," she added, then pressed the Send button.

She opened Beverly's first message. It was rather a short, typically friendly account of the church social she'd recently attended. In the next message, sent within a couple of hours of the previous one, she had added a few gossipy tidbits, then a question about what brand of yarn she should buy to make slippers.

"Hi Beverly. Any good quality worsted-weight yarn will do for slippers. Wish I could write a longer message, but I'm really busy right now crocheting my new signature piece. I'll be in touch as soon as I have a few extra minutes. Good luck. I know you'll do a great job. K."

She finished her tea, made sure the back door and all

the windows were locked, then grabbed her keys and purse and bat, and left to go buy sequins. She finally located them in a discount store across town. The shape and flatness of the sequins guaranteed easy placement and rearrangement without the bother of stitching them in place. She chose a box of silver ones and hurried back home.

When she returned home, her mind was so focused on making up for the hour she'd just lost that she hardly noticed Joe Vestal working outside on the front of his house. He paused and watched her, as if waiting for her to speak or approach. In her rush, she merely waved at him and hurried to her front door. Once inside, she tossed her purse and package on the love seat, hefted the bat, and toured the house, beginning with the living room and kitchen.

Every room was undisturbed, exactly as she had left it—until she stepped into the studio. The scene there froze her in horror.

For a moment, her mind refused to believe what her eyes saw. On the floor under the dressmaker's form, in an unraveled, tangled heap, lay the yarn that had formed the partially finished evening gown.

"What?" she gasped.

The trembling started somewhere in the middle of her body and worked its way to her extremities. Her knees gave way and she sank to the floor, unable to take her eyes from the unraveled dress.

Time slipped away. Kate had no idea how long she sat there, as addled and motionless as a stunned bird. At last, some sort of sensibility trickled into her, and she stirred. Like a grieving old woman, she struggled to her feet, then groped her way to the living room. She got her cellphone out of her purse and called Peter.

"Peter. Someone broke into my house again." She clamped her jaw, trying to stop her teeth from chattering.

"Kate? Are you all right?"

"Yes ... no ... I don't know ..." She began to sob.

"Are you in your house right now?"

"Yes," she squeaked.

"Are you alone?"

"Yes. B-but, Peter, my dress—"

"I'm on my way."

She collapsed on the floor again, this time weeping so hard she could barely breathe. In the periphery of her awareness, she heard her name, then knew someone was in the room with her. With effort she raised an unfocused gaze.

"Kate! Kate! It's Joe. Can you get up? Let me help you." She felt as lifeless as a sodden rag. "Take my hand," he said. His calloused fingers wrapped around hers. "Here. Nice and easy." With his other arm around her shoulder, Joe managed to get her to her feet. She swayed against him and clung to his hand.

"Thank you," she whispered, pressing her face to his chest. It felt so good to have a warm, strong body to support her.

"What's wrong, Kate? Are you sick?"

The image of the unraveled evening gown filled her mind. She shook her head, unable to speak.

"I believe you've been working so hard you've worn yourself out, and now you're exhausted." He peered at her face. "Listen, I have a fresh pot of coffee brewing over at my house. Let's go over there and have a cup. I even made a cake last night. It's just a box mix, but it's still cake. You can tell me what happened to get you in this state."

She found her voice. "No. Peter's coming."

Just then the strident shriek of sirens reached her.

"You called the police?" he asked, alarmed. "Why? What's happened, Kate?"

"Someone broke in." Her words came out coherently, but labored. "I need to sit."

He guided her to the love seat. She sank onto the soft cushions, closed her eyes and buried her face in her hands.

"Now, now," he said. "Don't cry. I'll go get you something to drink. OK? I'll be right back."

She nodded, not lifting her head or opening her eyes. She heard him leave.

A few moments later, her doorbell rang. "Sage Hills P.D.!"

Oh, it sounds like one of those awful shows on TV, she thought. I've turned my home and this neighborhood into a reality show.

With effort, she drew in a deep breath and pushed herself to her feet. The officer rang the bell again and once again announced his affiliation. She hoped it was Johnny. She trusted him. She felt safe with Johnny. He cared.

She reached the door and opened it. The middle-aged officer on the other side was no one she had seen before. "Please. Come inside."

"I'm Chez Parker with the Sage Hills Police Department. Detective Matthews with the Fort Worth P.D. called. He said there has been a break-in here."

"Yes."

He pulled on tight latex gloves as he shot a swift glance around the room. He turned to pin a flinty gaze on her.

"You want to tell me what happened?"

She wanted Peter to be there, not this unknown man.

"Someone got into my house while I was gone."

He examined the front door and the storm door, twisting the knobs, testing the locks. He strode to the back door and went through the same knob-shaking, lock-turning inspection.

"You leave your doors unlocked?" He gave her a sharp glance, then began examining windows.

"No. I double-check everything. I had to unlock the door when I came home."

He looked around. "Nothing seems disturbed in here. Did you straighten up?"

She shook her head.

The look he fastened on her was so hard and so prolonged that she squirmed as if she had committed a crime herself.

"Ma'am, if the doors were still locked when you got home, and you say nothing has been disturbed, what makes you think you've had a break-in?"

"I don't *think* there was a break-in. I *know* there was. Come with me," she said stiffly and led him to her studio. She stopped at the doorway, closed her eyes for a moment, then opened them and stepped inside.

"There." She pointed at the heap of unraveled yarn on the floor.

He stepped around her and frowned at the soft mound. He nudged it with the toe of his shiny black shoe. She started to yelp in protest, but stopped. He certainly couldn't hurt the dress at this point.

"What's this?" he asked.

"Kate?" Peter's voice preceded him down the hall. She turned gratefully and used all her resolve not to throw herself into his arms the way she had done the last time. What had happened today was far, far worse and much more sinister than finding a simple rose on her pillow.

"Thank you for coming," she said, curling and relaxing her hands. Why did her fingers feel so numb?

"Of course." For a moment, it seemed he was going to

take her in his arms anyway, but he didn't. "You know all you have to do is call. Now, what's going on?"

Some superficial but observant part of her mind noted his casual dress: simple white shirt with the sleeves rolled halfway up, blue jeans, boots. No badge anywhere to be seen, but his pistol was tucked into the holster at his waist.

"Is this your day off? Oh, Peter, I'm so sorry to bother you."

He gently grasped her upper arms and bent his head slightly to look into her eyes. She read his deep concern.

"Kate. It's fine. Tell me what happened."

"There. Right there on the floor." She turned to look at the soft heap of yarn. "Someone destroyed the evening dress I've been working on all week. Hours and hours and hours of work, and it's supposed to be done as soon as … and now, look at it …" Her voice cracked and she stopped speaking.

A frown descended across his handsome face, chasing away any trace of softness.

"When did this happen? Were you here?"

"No. I went to the store … well, several of them, actually, because I was looking for sequins, but the first two places …" She broke off, realizing she was blathering. "When I came home, the evening gown had been unpinned from the mannequin and unraveled. Look at it!" She pressed one hand to her lips, trying hard to neither shriek nor weep.

Strong Kate, Warrior Kate, she reminded herself.

"Was anyone in the house when you came inside?"

"No one."

Joe came into the room, a white mug in his hand. He ignored the uniformed officers and barely glanced at Peter as he handed it to Kate.

"I made some herbal tea instead of coffee for you," he said. "I thought it would be more calming."

Peter never took his eyes off the man, nor did he smile.

"Thank you, Joe." Kate took the mug from him and gratefully sipped. It was minty and sweet, calming and refreshing at the same time. "That is so good. Just what I need."

Joe's face creased into a smile, but the worry never left his features.

"Let's you and me go talk," Peter said, laying a hand on Joe's shoulder.

"Peter?" Kate said, starting to trail after them as Peter more or less herded Joe out of the room.

"Ma'am," Officer Parker said, stopping her, "have you seen anyone suspicious hanging around the neighborhood?"

She was overcome with a sudden flash of light-headedness that caused her to sway.

"Hey there!" he said, catching her arm. "You all right?"

"It's just ... You know that feeling of having done this before?"

"Déjà vu?"

"Exactly."

"Here, let's go into the other room and you sit down." He gently led her down the short hallway and into the living room. Right then, she clung to him, not liking how the room seemed to pitch and tilt. Peter and Joe were at the far end of the kitchen, talking quietly. They stood nearly head to head, facing each other. Peter's granite expression never changed; Joe looked earnest but nervous.

No wonder, Kate thought. *A big tough cop in your face would make anyone twitchy.* She couldn't help but hope Peter would not be rough on Joe. The old man was only trying to be a good neighbor.

When she was settled on the love seat, the warm mug between her hands, the officer poised his pen above his notebook and asked, "Now, have you seen anyone suspicious in the neighborhood?"

She shook her head. "No. I talked about all this before. Do we really have go over it again?"

"I'm afraid so. Have you received any strange phone calls?"

Again she shook her head. "No." She looked over his shoulder at the two men in the kitchen. "Why is Peter grilling Joe?"

"He's just talking to him, ma'am. We've got a report you filed about a missing portfolio. What's that?"

"I kept all my sketches in it." She repeated the events related to losing the portfolio. "I suppose no one has turned it in?"

"I don't think so, ma'am."

He scribbled a few notes while another officer finished dusting for fingerprints. In the meantime, Joe left without saying a word to her.

"We'll be on our way now, ma'am," Officer Parker said, "unless you can think of anything else."

She met his eyes and felt the full impact of how futile the entire situation was. Unless they found fingerprints other than hers, she was pretty sure the investigation was over. She shook her head and dropped her gaze to the empty mug in her hands.

"Thank you," she said quietly, and they left.

Peter went into the kitchen and started making coffee as if he were a frequent visitor to the place.

"What about fingerprints?" she asked him. "Someone took them the other night and again today. I guess if they'd found any ...."

"You're a good housekeeper, Kate," he said, pouring water into the coffeemaker. "I hope you didn't wipe everything off after either break-in because only one set of prints showed up and they were yours."

"I didn't wipe anything. Does that mean whoever broke in wore gloves?"

"I'd say so. Unless you left the rose there yourself, and I'm sure you didn't."

"Of course not!"

"Kate, you're not going to get any help from Sage Hills P.D. over the loss of your property. There was a homicide on the other side of town early this morning, and that's where the focus and manpower is going to be."

"A murder?" She got up and carried the empty mug into the kitchen.

"Yes."

"Sage Hills is so small that it's frightening to think of murder here." She shuddered. "A damaged dress fades in comparison."

"It has to be that way. But I'm going to help you."

"But Sage Hills is not your jurisdiction." She laid her hand on his arm and searched his eyes. "You can't do that ... can you?"

"I'm doing it on my own. I have some days off, so ...."

"That's very generous of you, Peter, but I don't expect you to use your leisure time doing some sort of freelance investigation on my behalf."

He smiled and brushed her cheek with his fingertip. "Why don't you sit down and see if you can relax? I'd like to talk to you."

She rinsed Joe's mug, but instead of putting it in the drainer, she gazed at it for a moment. Inexpensive and plain, probably purchased from a bargain store, it wasn't very attractive, but simple and comforting. She dried it off and set it on the counter so she wouldn't forget to return it.

"Did you chase Joe away?" she said, not looking at Peter.

The coffee gurgled, and he turned to lean against the

cabinet, arms folded across his broad chest.

"Why do you ask?"

"Because he was here, he brought me tea, he talked to you, and he left without saying goodbye." She looked at him. "What did you say to him, Peter?"

He shrugged as if dismissing her curiosity. "Not a lot. We talked about what happened to your property. I asked him if he'd noticed any odd or suspicious activity over here."

"And?"

"He said the old woman on the other side of him has been causing you a lot of trouble. Has she?"

"A bit, yes."

Peter lifted one eyebrow. "Care to elaborate?"

"We've been over this more than once."

"Let's go over it again."

"I told you about her. Frieda Mahl, the neighborhood eccentric. I saw her digging in Joe's backyard—well it wasn't Joe's when she did it. She didn't like it when I went to see what she'd been doing."

"She threatened you?"

"No. As I said before, she just waved her arms around and yelled."

He seemed lost in his thoughts for a little bit, then turned to take a couple of cups from the cabinet as if he had done it a thousand times.

"What about Joe?" he asked.

"What about him?"

"Do you know he has a thing for you?"

Kate felt her eyes get big. "What? Oh, he does not. I mean ... well, I suppose he might."

"Hey. *I* have a thing for you, so I recognize it on the faces of other guys who feel the same."

She felt a blush warm her face and tried to ignore it.

"Joe is sixty-five, if he's a day!"

"So?"

"Well, Adam is about that old. Does Adam have a thing for me too?"

"We'll get to Adam in a minute."

Kate plopped down in a chair at the table and gaped up at the tall Texas detective who could make her heart skip a beat or two.

"What do you mean, 'We'll get to Adam in a minute'?"

"I mean, we'll talk about him after you tell me what you know about Joe."

Kate sighed. She leaned sideways a bit to look at the coffeemaker behind him. "I probably need coffee first."

He filled both cups and settled across the table from her. She did her best not to think about his eyes or his smile, or how warm and safe she felt in his presence.

"Joe is a nice guy. He's married, he has a son, he's retired. He's nearly blind."

"Married, you say?"

"Yes! With a son."

"Have you met his wife and son?"

She shook her head. "He told me his wife will move in when the house is ready. I've never even seen the son, so I don't think he lives with Joe."

"You haven't asked?"

"It's none of my business, Peter."

"If he's nearly blind, why doesn't he wear glasses?"

"He said he used to wear them, but they don't help. Cataracts."

"Hmm. So how can he renovate the house?"

She refused to say she'd wondered the same thing. "He's

not completely blind, obviously. He can see to get around."

"Yeah. And not cut off a finger with a power saw."

Kate crimped her lips.

"Where'd he live before he moved to Sage Hills?"

"I don't know."

Peter gazed at her without speaking for a minute. "What *do* you know about the man, Kate?"

"I know he's very nice," she said stiffly. "He's lonely and kind and ... and ..." Her voice trailed.

"You see my point."

She maintained silence. Of course Peter had a point, but Joe had been so kind, watching out for her, checking on her.

"Has Joe ever said anything to you that you'd consider odd or threatening in any way?"

"Of course not!" She paused, then added, "Not odd or threatening, you understand, but he did seem to take my need to get back to work too personally. He's wanted me to go over to his house for tea or coffee, and he's wanted to take me out for breakfast. I've tried to explain that I had to work. Well, I guess it hurt his feelings, as if I were rejecting him. I promised we'd go to Sunday brunch tomorrow."

"What about Frieda?" Peter said. "Tell me about some of her bizarre behavior."

"She was scattering dried sage in my yard this morning."

Peter gave no reaction, as if this were a common occurrence.

"I understand sage is used for driving away evil spirits," Kate continued. "I think she thinks I'm evil, and she wants me to leave Hawkins Drive."

"I find that hard to believe. That anyone would think you're evil, I mean."

"Maybe you should ask her why she did it. I would, but I can't get her to come to the door."

"You may rest assured, I'll be talking to her." He took a sip of his coffee. "Tell me this. Do you think Frieda might have come into your house and unraveled your dress?"

Kate took in a deep breath and blew it out.

"Maybe. I just can't think that anyone other than a crazy person would do such a thing. But I don't know how she would get in here." She leaned forward. "Honestly, Peter, I've been so careful to make sure the doors and windows are locked. And according to that officer, no one has broken in."

Peter's gaze traveled to the kitchen door leading outside.

"The locks on your doors are the easiest kind to pick. You should get new ones. And have deadbolts installed also."

"I'm sure you're right." She squelched her sigh and sipped her coffee.

"And some security lights," he added. "The motion sensor types."

"Whoever broke in here and left the rose and unraveled the evening dress came into this house in broad daylight. Lights wouldn't have done any good."

"That's true, but it's a good idea to have those lights anyway." Left unsaid was the notion that someone might try to get into her house after dark. "Installing a security camera would be a good idea too."

"I'm sure it would." She did not bother to mention the expense of these items; she was still waiting for that advance on her first book. "You don't think that Frieda or whoever came in through a window, do you?"

"Nothing is impossible. I think it's more likely the person used a credit card or a lock pick and came in through the door. Probably the back door since it was light outside."

"Oh dear," she said faintly.

"Tell me about Adam," he said, changing the subject so abruptly that she blinked.

"You've met him. He's my agent; he used to write for magazines, and now he owns a small literary agency."

"I've met him, but I mean tell me *about* him."

She frowned. "He's older, late sixties. A widower with no kids. Hardworking, driven to succeed. He's kind and rather fatherly. What else do you want to know?" She narrowed her eyes. "You don't think he's the one who broke in, do you? Or stole my sketches?"

"I'm just asking questions, Kate. It's how my brain is wired. Everyone is a person of interest."

"And you're always on the job."

"That's right. Where is his agency located?"

"He has an office in his home."

"Where's that?"

"Why, Peter! Surely you aren't going to go question my agent, are you?"

"Yes I am, Kate."

"Oh, but don't you understand that Adam would have nothing to gain by ruining my work? If I can't work or meet deadlines, I'll lose my contract. I won't make any money, and if I don't, neither will Adam. Fifteen percent of nothing is nothing."

This statement apparently failed to impress Peter, because he said, "Do you think he might have taken your sketches?"

His words stunned her into complete silence.

"Why would he?" she said when she found her voice. "Weren't you listening? What possible reason would Adam Vargas have to swipe my work when he's trying to sell it?" She scowled at Peter. "Is this what makes a detective? Looking at people and facts by turning everything upside down and backward?"

"Sometimes that's what we have to do to shake loose secrets."

"Well, I don't like suspecting my friends!" she huffed.

"I understand how you feel, and I'm sorry, but the world isn't always a pretty place. Now, tell me about your ex-husband."

Another abrupt change. "What about him?"

She read Peter's expression as one of patience beginning to strain.

"Are you friendly?"

"We get along. And if you think Harry did this—"

"I'm looking at everyone. Please understand that."

"Are you going to look at Vanessa too?" She jumped up and paced around the room. "Maybe go up to Maine and confront all the women of the Hook and Needle Club?"

"I might need to talk to some of your daughter's friends. And have any of these women from the Hook and Needle Club been to Sage Hills in the last few days?"

She stopped pacing long enough to gape at him, then all but stomped her foot. She resumed her agitated path up and down the room.

Peter pushed back his chair and got to his feet. She ignored how nicely his strong frame looked in her kitchen.

"What about this fellow who was stalking you online?"

"I haven't heard a word from him."

"He hasn't called?"

"No. No one but my close friends and family have my number."

"Has he sent you any more emails?"

"Nothing."

"Any more upsetting comments or chatter?"

"I closed down my accounts and haven't signed up for new ones."

He looked at her for a long minute. His face gave no indication of what was on his mind. He turned on his heel and walked to the door.

"Where are you going?"

"I'll talk to you later, Kate," he said. "Keep your doors locked."

"But ... are you coming back?"

"I have a few personal errands to run. I'll talk to you later."

When cooler heads prevail, I assume, she thought peevishly. *Particularly mine.*

Nineteen

Shoving away all thoughts of Peter, she checked her locks, then propped a kitchen chair under each doorknob. For a time, she stared down at the inefficient lock on her back door, thinking of the ease with which someone could come inside. Both locks had to be replaced, and soon.

She opened her laptop, and when it booted up, she typed "locksmith Sage Hills" into the search bar. Within fifteen minutes she had called every locksmith listed. None of them wanted to come out on a Saturday, so she made an appointment for Monday afternoon to get new locks and deadbolts.

For a moment, Kate sat on the love seat, her face in her hands, feeling lower than she had in a while. She had offended Joe. She had worried Vanessa. Frieda was trying to magically cast her out of the neighborhood. Paige was tied up at Once Upon a Yarn. Vivi was working at the hotel, and Mary Beth was far away. She wallowed in her misery for a while, and finally realized what she was doing.

"What a pity party!" she said aloud, dropping her hands and sitting up straight. Feeling sorry for herself and lingering in the pit of despair had never been the solution to any problem.

She stood up, brushed the metaphorical dust from her hands and the cobwebs from her brain, and marched into her studio. Without pausing to feel sick all over again from the sight of her unraveled dress, she settled on the floor next to it, and sought the end of the yarn. With deliberation and gentleness, she began to wind the yarn in a ball, careful not to tangle any of it.

Kate got home from church Sunday afternoon, thinking about Joe. She had not eaten Sunday brunch with him as promised, but she wasn't sure he would even speak with her. Vivi's blue Mini Cooper was in her carport, and the moment Kate stopped her van, Vivi was trotting across the street. Kate met her, carrying her purse and her bat.

"I'm so happy to see you!" Vivi hollered, giving Kate a hug. "I feel like I've been in a wringer and stretched beyond all measure."

Clumsily, Kate returned the hug, knocking the tip of the bat into Vivi's thighs.

"What's this?" Vivi said. "You playing softball in Sunday School now?"

Kate laughed. "No. But after everything that's happened this week, I take it with me when I go so I'll have it in hand when I come back."

Vivi blinked. "My goodness, girl! What's happened?"

"Come on in, and I'll tell you all about it. You can stay for lunch if you don't mind tuna salad and potato chips."

As they walked through the house, looking in every corner and closet, bat aloft in Kate's hands, she related what had happened.

"Mercy!" Vivi said as she sat down at the kitchen table. "Kate, I am so sorry I wasn't here for you. Why didn't you call me, or at least send me a text?"

Kate met her eyes. "For one thing, you hate my text messages—"

"Well, they are a bit like reading a letter from my mother."

"Oh hush that," Kate laughed. "And another thing, you were up-to-your-eyeballs busy at work. There is no way I'd ever lay my problems on you when you are that busy. Ever."

Vivi's eyes softened, and she smiled. "Kate Stevens. Honest to goodness. You're one in a million. But I'm your friend, and if you go through something like this again, you better call me. I will always spare time for you."

Monday afternoon, the locksmith installed new locks on both doors. They were now as secure as locks, deadbolts and keys could make them.

Over the last two days, she had also rewound all the unraveled thread and had settled down to start the project again. The first flush of creative energy had been spent when she'd worked on the dress the first time. It seemed to Kate the endeavor was turning stale. But she refused to stop working on it and turn to a different project. Her years of crocheting had taught her the only way to build a collection of garments was to push through, even in those rare instances when she found herself becoming bored or disillusioned. More than ever, she needed to hold steadfast to her commitment. Anyone who would see this finished project would never know this was the second attempt.

Shortly after the locksmith left, her doorbell chimed. When she opened it, Joe stood on her stoop. With his thinning brown hair mussed, his face florid, and his clothes wrinkled, he looked distracted and on edge. Concern shot through her immediately.

"What's wrong, Joe?"

"It's my wife," he said. "A friend back home called just a few minutes ago and said she's had a stroke."

"A stroke. I'm so sorry to hear that."

"Thank you for saying so. I wanted to let you know I am going to be gone for a while."

"Of course. Are you leaving right now?"

"Yes. The other day, I told that cop, the big burly one—your boyfriend—that I'd keep an eye on things and make sure Frieda doesn't create any more havoc for you, but I can't do that now."

"Please, don't worry about me. I have new locks. See?" She pointed to the doorknob. "And my bat is never out of reach. You need to get to your wife and take care of her. Let me know what you find out, OK? Here, I'll give you my cellphone number." She got a pen from her purse and tore a scrap of paper off the back of an envelope. She scribbled down her number and handed it to him. "Now you call me, OK? I want to know how she is, and how you're doing."

He tucked the paper in his shirt pocket. "I will, thank you."

"Your son is driving you, I assume?"

"How's that?"

"Your son? He's taking you?"

"Yes, yes, of course."

"Good luck. I'll say a prayer for you both."

"Thank you, Kate."

He hurried away. He'd been so busy, preparing the house for his wife, and now this devastating news. Kate went back into the house, her heart aching. She offered a prayer for her new neighbor and for his wife.

After a quick breakfast Tuesday morning, Kate settled into her comfy Queen Anne chair and worked with single-minded intent on reconstructing the evening dress until lunchtime. She paused only long enough to eat a peanut butter sandwich and an apple with a glass of milk.

By late afternoon, she'd put it away for the day. She had made good progress, but maybe she'd pushed herself a little too hard. Her hands ached and her neck was stiff. A good long soak in a warm bath before bed would make her feel better. She would have taken a walk, but the sun was low in the sky by then. She harbored no desire to be outside after dark.

She turned on her laptop and saw several new emails from Beverly.

"You certainly know how to make someone feel special," Beverly had written in her first, short message. Kate smiled, feeling good—until she read the next sentence: *"I pour my heart out to you, share with you the happenings of my life, but you brush me off because you are 'too busy.' I get more attention from my television."*

Kate blinked. This terse, unhappy note was nothing like Beverly's usual friendly messages.

She opened the woman's next email, one sentence long: *"Fair-weather friend, as defined in my dictionary: A friend who is a friend only when it's convenient or profitable."*

The third message read, *"The very least you could do is take a minute to tell me hello."*

The last message turned her blood cold: *"DON'T YOU DARE LEAVE ME AGAIN!"*

Kate stared at the screen, her eyes so wide they ached.

The high-pitched ringing in her ears deafened her until she finally caught her breath. This made no sense. None at all, unless ....

"How could it be?" she whispered, one hand to her mouth. Surely Nick Scott had not pretended to be Beverly. Had he? But he must have. The tone of these emails matched the messages she received from Nick. And the final message mirrored one he had sent to her. Kate jerked back, then closed her laptop and stared at it as if it were a poisonous viper. Finally, she turned away. *What should I do now?*

She sat for a long time while the events of the last few weeks roiled through her mind like the floodwaters of a muddy river.

She lifted her head and dropped her hands to her lap. So what if Beverly turned out to be whoever Nick Scott was? So what if this awful person spewed unkind, even vile comments about her? Those nasty remarks did not define Kate Stevens, and eventually they'd fade away. If she lived her life with honesty, kindness, and integrity, if she moved forward rather than slinking back to hide in the shadows, if she remained strong, she would overcome this situation.

She would call Adam in the morning and tell him what was going on, and she'd get in touch with Peter. Surely in all his years of investigating, he'd met someone who could track down the identity of this awful person who had, for whatever reason, chosen to stalk her online. There had to be some kind of law that would put a stop to it all.

Kate's cellphone rang just as she reached her front door, checking to make sure the new locks were thrown.

"Hello?"

"Kate? It's Joe."

"Hi! How are you? Have you seen your wife yet?"

"No, I'm not with her yet, but something tells me everything is going to be all right."

"That's a great way to think!" she said. "I am keeping you both in my prayers."

"That's sweet of you, Kate. I'm afraid I must ask a favor of you."

"Sure. What do you need?"

"I was in such a rush when I left that I think I may have left my television on. Would you go over to my house and check?"

"I'd be happy to do that for you, but how can I get in?"

"There is a key to the front door in the watering can in the carport."

She grabbed up her bat and keys and went outside. The door locked behind her when it shut.

"OK. I'm on my way to your house even as we speak," she said, "so put your mind at rest."

"I'll do my best."

"Take care of yourself, Joe."

"Thank you. I will. I'll talk to you later."

She slid the phone into her pocket, but it rang again just as she reached Joe's carport.

"Hi there," Peter said. "I hope you aren't busy this evening."

A sweet flare of anticipation stirred.

"Well, right now I'm going to Joe's to make sure he turned off his television. He had an emergency and left so suddenly, he couldn't remember if he turned it off or not."

A short silence followed, then Peter said, "Kate, I know he's your neighbor, and you like him, but there is something about that guy I don't trust."

She laughed softly. "I think your job has made you suspect everyone."

She found the key exactly where Joe had said it was and walked to his front door.

"Not everyone. Not you. Would I ask a suspect if she'd like to go with me for an old-fashioned burger and fries this evening? There's this little retro diner I thought you might enjoy."

"I like retro."

"I thought you would. Which is why I usually call you instead of texting you. Do you realize you are the only person I know who texts in complete sentences?"

She laughed as she inserted the key into the door and turned the lock.

"I guess I'm just an old-fashioned girl. Vanessa rolls her eyes every time I—"

A screech behind her cut off her words just as she stepped through the doorway.

"Get out of there!"

She was so startled, she dropped the bat as she whirled to see Frieda standing on the walkway to Joe's front door. Frieda held her arms out behind her like unfurled chicken wings.

"Get out of there!" the woman yelled again. "Get out, get out, get out! I'll call the cops on *you* for a change! See how *you* like it!"

"It's OK, Frieda," Kate said as soothingly as she could. "Joe asked me to turn off his television."

"He can turn off his own television!"

Frieda was so agitated and loud that the woman who lived in the house next door to Vivi stepped outside to stare at them. If Frieda kept screaming, the entire neighborhood would be outside, and if they all liked her as much Vivi indicated, Kate would be the neighborhood pariah.

"What's going on?" Peter said.

"It's just Frieda hollering because I'm going into Joe's house. She's protective of the neighborhood. Remember? I told you that earlier. I'll call you back when I get home."

"Is everything all right?" She heard the concern in his voice.

"Yes, it's fine. No need to worry. I just need to calm her down. Talk to you in a bit." Kate pressed the End key and tucked the phone into her front pants pocket. She faced the wild-eyed woman who, at the moment, was tugging on her own hair as if to pull it out.

"Don't do that, Frieda. It's all right, truly. I'm just going to turn off the television, then I'm going back home."

The woman jumped back, still holding her arms behind her like jutting, folded wings.

"Don't call the cops on *me*. Don't you do it, don't you do it! You call the cops on the guilty party!"

What guilty party? Was it possible the woman knew who'd broken into Kate's house?

She stepped off the porch, and Frieda jumped back again, then started backing away.

"Wait! I'd like to talk to you."

But the woman fled across the lawn and darted into her own house. Kate looked across the street to see that she was under the watchful eye of several neighbors.

"It's all right," she called to them. "I'm just checking to be sure he turned off his television."

They broke apart and went toward their own homes. She went back to the front door and stepped inside.

Joe's house was like all the others on Hawkins Drive, small, economical, efficient. The curtains were drawn, making the living room quite dark. She glanced around and noticed, even in the gloom, the spotless appearance of everything. But where was the television?

"Well, for goodness' sake," she said, frowning. Then she heard the low sound of voices and realized the TV was in one of the bedrooms. She followed the sound down the hall where every door stood open except the one where the voices came from. She wrapped her fingers around the knob and turned.

The moment she opened the door, Kate realized she should have listened to Frieda and never entered Joe's house.

Twenty

"Well, well. At long last. Kate Stevens, step into my parlor."

The room was dark but for the light of one dim lamp and a computer screen where an animated video was playing. In that light, she saw that Joe Vestal's lined face had lost its fatherly warmth and caught shadows with eerie precision. He sat in a swivel desk chair in front of a long folding table cluttered with a computer, a printer, and several books and magazines.

"What are you doing here, Joe?"

"I live here."

"But ... your wife ...."

Joe ran his gaze slowly along her length. "My wife *is* here."

Fear wrapped tentacles around every bone, muscle, and tendon in her body. She backed toward the hallway, feeling helpless, wanting only to leave the awful house and the presence of someone who had been transformed into something sinister and unknown.

But before she could set one foot outside the open bedroom door, Joe leaped from his chair and grabbed her arm. His strength stunned her. Kate stared at him and looked into those eyes, for the first time seeing their clarity.

She swallowed hard. "You ... you don't have cataracts, do you, Joe?"

"No. I have twenty-twenty vision, and I don't have arthritis or breathing problems or any other affliction of the aged. I'm not hard of hearing. I'm healthier than most men half my age."

"Where's your wife?"

"I told you, my wife is here." He paused, and the smile he gave her caused a chill to slither down her spine. "In fact, she's standing right beside me."

"I don't understand," she whispered.

But that was a lie. She understood all too well that her good neighbor Joe had built a strange fantasy that included her as his leading lady. She wished she hadn't dropped her bat.

"Come here, my love," he said quietly, pulling her across the room to the long table. He pointed to the swivel chair in which he'd been sitting. "Sit there, and we'll talk."

She sat. The vinyl was still warm from his body. She cringed.

"How about a cup of tea?" Before she could reply, he added, "You've put off having tea with me so many times that now we'll have to make up for lost time."

She blinked up at him, at the smile that seemed frozen on his face but never reached his eyes. They had had such good rapport before that maybe she could reach some level of sense in him now.

"Tell me what's going on, Joe," she said in as reasonable a tone as possible. He chuckled and patted her on the head like a pet dog.

"You stay right here, and I'll go fix our tea." His gaze traveled across her carefully, as if looking for something in particular. He focused on her pants pocket, then held out one hand. "You have an itchy trigger finger when it comes to calling the cops, so give me the phone. I can see the outline of it, so ..." He made a beckoning gesture with his fingers.

She stared at him, trying to think of way to distract him, but he took a step closer. "You can hand it to me, or I can get it myself."

"No!" she gasped. "Here." She fumbled a moment, then pulled out the phone and handed it to him.

He grinned and placed it in the breast pocket of his shirt.

"You can't get out of this house, not without me seeing you, so don't try. I'd rather not get rough with you, Kate. Besides, we need to have a nice long chat."

He walked out the door, and as soon as she heard dishes rattling in the kitchen, she jumped up from the chair. His house had only front and back doors. Both could be seen from the kitchen, so she could not leave without being caught. She reached across the desk and pulled back the dark curtains, hoping to open the window and slip out. To her dismay, she saw narrow planks had been nailed across it on the inside. The cracks between the planks were far enough apart that she could see twilight, but not nearly wide enough to permit her even to fit her hand between them.

Were all the windows boarded up? Was that what all the sawing and hammering had been when she'd believed he'd been fixing up the house for his wife? Why hadn't she noticed these boarded windows from the outside?

She grabbed a board, but could only manage to grip with the tips of her fingers. She tried to tug it but it didn't budge. She stepped back, frustrated, her fear growing by the minute.

"I hope you aren't thinking of leaving," he said right behind her. She whirled. He held two cups. "You always want to leave me, Katie. Or give me the dregs of your time. You seem to think that's enough. This time, you stay."

He thrust a cup into her hands. She felt she might be sick if she were to take even a small sip.

"I don't know what you're talking about."

"Of course you do. You constantly brush me off. You have

no time for me, ever. Think of all those occasions when you've dismissed me with hardly more than a passing thought."

She stared at him, trying to make sense of the situation.

"I'm sorry if I've made you feel that way. Truly I am. I thought you understood how busy I've been. It wasn't that I didn't want to have coffee or tea with you—"

"Well, you don't have a choice now," he said. He pointed at the desk chair. "Sit there and stay put. Like a good girl." She hesitated, and he leaned near her face. "Do it, Kate. Now."

She sat. He sipped his tea, then nodded toward her cup. "Drink."

He gave her his hard stare. Had he added something to the tea that would make her pass out? She must stay lucid and figure out a way to get away from him. She pretended to sip. Joe said nothing, but his gaze never wavered from her. What did he want? What did he plan to do to her? Why was he so resentful of her when they barely knew each other? They had seemed to be on friendly terms from the day he arrived with the real estate agent. Surely there was a way to reach him now, to soften him.

"It's so hard to see this change in you," she said. "I thought we were becoming friends."

He chuffed. "We were friends several weeks ago, but you have put a stop to that at every turn." He lifted his cup and drank, his eyes still on hers.

"Joe, we haven't known each other that long."

He was shaking his head before she'd finished speaking. "We've known each other since late July, so don't give me that."

"What? Why, we haven't!"

He barked a laugh without a trace of humor. "Allow me to prove to you …."

He bent over the computer keyboard and tapped keys. The screen filled.

"There." He spun the chair to face the desk, angled the monitor toward her a couple of inches and stepped aside. "I archived everything."

Kate scooted forward to see the words, then fell back as if she'd been shoved. She gaped at paragraph after paragraph of the chats she had had with Nick Scott, beginning with the very first query she'd put on the old car forum.

"What ...?" she said, her horrified gaze fixed on the screen.

"Take a good long look at that. Recognize it? Scroll down."

"But—"

"Do it!"

His voice sent ice surging through her blood. Watching the words speed past made her dizzy.

"Stop. Look."

She did as he said. It took a moment for her eyes to adjust to the still screen. Then, she saw every conversation, every email she had shared with Beverly Amos.

She turned to him slowly.

"Why, Kate, I'm a handsome young guy who thinks you're terrific. And I'm a sweet guy who restores classic cars for a hobby. And I'm also just a lonely, elderly widow with fur babies who believes you can never have too much yarn." He gave her a wry grin. "I nearly messed up with Beverly when I mentioned grandchildren, didn't I? But lucky for me I can think on my feet. Close call, that one."

The veil had lifted from that dark secret, and bit by bit, she knew the reality of what had happened. Her stunned gaze blurred and a high-pitched sound rang in her ears. She swayed in the chair, but Joe grabbed her.

"Steady on, there! No fainting allowed."

Her vision cleared, and her hearing returned to normal. Kate closed her eyes and opened them slowly, gathering her wits.

"You're Nick."

"I am."

"You're also Beverly."

He chuckled. "At your service, my dear."

"And you're the one who broke into my house, aren't you?"

"Not hard to do, but you *would* change the locks. And you can blame the crazy lady next door for that."

Joe and Frieda were in cahoots? Surely not.

"For whatever reason, she left that rose on your doorstep. When I saw it, it seemed to me a grand gesture would be to leave one on your pillow."

She shut her eyes again, slowly. Deliberately. *Please, God, let this be a dream.*

But it wasn't. Joe stood so near to her that she could hear his breathing and feel his body heat. She hated these sensations, and she tried to scoot away. He clamped a beefy hand on the chair back.

"Too bad I had to unravel that dress you were making, but my darling, it was stealing you away from me."

Kate was sure she would be sick at any moment. She pressed her fist to her lips.

"In all honesty, Kate, I'm sorry the situation had to reach this point. All this nonsense—this trickery—could have been avoided if you had just let me send you a gift. You see, that gift would have been something to show you that I was falling in love with you, sight unseen. My plan was eventually to reveal to you that I wasn't the handsome guy in that photo I used; that was just a stock photo I found online. I figured once you knew how much I cared, as more than a friend, you'd forgive me for being middle-aged and not very good-looking."

He pushed out a slow breath.

"That was my plan. But I've always believed in having backup plans to get what I want." He gave her a sharp look. "You might want to keep that in mind for future reference."

He paused, waiting for his words to sink in. "You weren't hard to find, especially once Beverly tricked you into revealing where you lived. Sage Hills is small enough that finding your home was easy. A man of my ingenuity—forgive me if I sound boastful—had no trouble working out a deal for the vacant house next door."

"Oh my," she said, her voice faint. No other words would form, and she could only gape at him.

"I must take care of you. In fact, it is my mission to take care of you. Come with me."

He held out one hand. When she did not move, he reached out and clasped hers, pulling her to her feet.

"Don't be afraid, Kate. It's a good thing."

He led her across the hall and opened a door.

"Ladies first," he said, guiding her across the threshold into a dark room. "I can feel your tension, my love. Don't be afraid."

Still gripping her hand, he took a few steps and switched on a lamp. The room glowed in the soft light to reveal a double bed with a blue spread, a small bedside table, and a dresser. "This will be your room for now. I'm still working on ours."

Ours? She tried not to let alarm show in her eyes.

"But here, Katie-girl. This is what I want you to see. This is what has taken the longest to prepare for you." He turned her to face the other side of the room where he had built a full-length system of shelves, drawers and cubbyholes. Yarn and thread filled the spaces. New crochet hooks in all sizes and colors winked in the golden lamplight.

"Paige Bryant is such a lovely woman," he said. "I noticed it right away, the time I brought that note for her to give to you."

Kate had no words. She could only stare at him, wondering when this nightmare would end.

"Paige was so eager to please that I decided her shop would be the beneficiary of my business. I told her I wanted to outfit a crochet studio as a surprise for my wife, and she was so helpful in suggesting all manner of articles. She assured me you'd love it all. Do you?"

Kate found her voice. "You talked to Paige? You told her you were shopping for me?"

He laughed softly. "Not to worry. I did not mention your name, or mine." He whispered, "Our secret is safe. In fact, I took care that she would never see me as you do. A fake mustache—it looks very real—a pair of discount store eyeglasses, a few extra layers of clothes to add girth, an old baseball cap pulled low. Paige would never recognize me as the man you see before you."

She felt sicker than ever. Joe led her to the built-in unit and ran his free hand over the smooth wood, smiling as he picked up a skein of yarn, then laid it down.

"I'm sorry I ruined that fancy dress you were making," he said. "I was so angry when you brushed me off, pleading lack of time, but you seemed to have plenty of time to go traipsing off to shop. Unraveling those stitches felt so good. I hope you understand and forgive me. I promise I won't do that again. There won't be a reason for me to destroy your work. You'll be here, spending all your time with me."

Spending all my time with him? I can't. What have I done to deserve this? Dear God, please get me out of here.

"I ordered a nice comfy chair for you," he said, "but it won't be here for another month. It's custom-made." He smiled as if his words and this room were the most altruistic gift ever bestowed.

I'd rather die than be trapped here. She almost said these words aloud, but stopped. She had a feeling Joe harbored a hot temper and a short fuse.

"Best of all, look what I have." He opened a drawer and pulled out her leather portfolio. "Here it is! You shouldn't leave your van unlocked. Not if you carry your valuables with you. But," he smiled broadly, "this will all be yours again."

She stared at it. "You took my portfolio."

"Didn't you just hear me say I gave that note to Paige? Of course I took it."

"But why? It was so important to me."

The insanity in his eyes burned like flames of a wildfire. "Don't you think I know that? I wanted to make you hurt like you hurt me. Just to let you know how it felt. Oh, and another thing, Kate. The way I've fixed the windows in this room—which is the only room you will be living in until I finish our master suite—no one will be able to peer in from the outside and see you. Those mini blinds really don't offer complete privacy. I should know. I watched you through yours often enough."

She turned her face away from his gaze. How could she have been so foolish as to trust this man? How had he deceived her? Peter had known there was something odd about Joe. What signs had Peter seen that she had missed?

"Let's go back to my office, shall we?" Joe said, tugging gently on her arm. "We still have some things to discuss."

He led her back to the room and seated her again, then pulled up a chair to face her. He reached for his tea, looked into the cup, then lifted his head. His face was impassive, but his eyes cold.

"One thing you must remember, Kate."

"What's that?" she managed to whisper.

"Don't try to get away. Ever." He paused, giving her time to think about it. "Stay right there while I get us some more tea. Do not move, not so much as the twitch of an eyelash."

He got her cup, frowned and said, "I guess I should put more sugar in it for you, shouldn't I? Maybe I'll get it right this time." He left the room.

I have to get out of here. If I can just get to the ball bat, I have a chance. She jumped up but tripped over the leg of the chair Joe had pulled out for himself. It crashed to the floor. She scrambled to her feet, but Joe was there almost immediately.

He lifted her with both arms from behind.

"Where are you going, Kate?"

"I ... I don't know."

"What did I say twenty seconds ago? *Don't try to get away. Ever.*"

She struggled, but his iron grip held her fast. She shrieked, trying to kick, but he lifted her easily, and she flailed her legs against air. He carried her like that across the room to the desk chair. Kate butted her head backward. Pain shot through her skull, and she knew she'd connected with some part of him. He growled and tightened his grip until she could barely breathe.

"Stop fighting me," he said. "Stop it!"

The warmth of his blood dripped onto her shirt and wetted her back. If she wounded him severely enough, surely he'd loosen his hold. Screaming, she jerked her head back again and kicked backward, hitting nothing.

"Quiet!" he roared. He grabbed up an old paper towel and crammed it into her mouth. She tried to spit it out, but the paper clung to her lips, the insides of her cheeks, and her tongue.

He plunked her down in the chair, then spun it around and shoved it into the kneehole of the desk. He held it in place with his torso, yanking her arms behind the chair. She struggled and tried to yell, but the paper nearly strangled her.

Holding her wrists with one hand, he reached into the clutter on the desk and grabbed a roll of duct tape. She heard the tape rip. He grabbed the wad of wet paper out of her mouth and pressed the tape across her lips before she could scream.

It ripped again and he strapped her wrists together. She screamed behind the tape, making little sound. She tried to kick in the small space beneath the desk, shoving against the wall with both feet.

Joe easily blocked her efforts with his body. Still pressed against the back of the chair, he bent and grabbed one kicking foot. He taped it to the base of the chair, then did the same with the other. When he finished, he pulled the chair away from the desk and spun it to face him. He looked down at her. He was sweating and breathing hard. Blood smeared across his cheek and chin and still oozed from the lip she had split when she'd head-butted him. Kate was gratified to know she had made solid contact.

"You're stronger than you look, but you're no match for a man. Especially one who was the pride of his college football team." He grinned as though he thought she'd be proud of him. "I didn't want to have to do all this, but you forced my hand."

Twenty-One

Kate knew she was trapped, but a part of her screamed in her brain, *Warrior Kate fights back!*

As if he could read her mind, Joe grabbed her face in one hand.

"I have an entire roll of duct tape, but I'd rather not use it. I have fists, and I don't want to use them either. I'm a peaceable man. But I will use tape and fists if you force me to. It's up to you."

She blinked at him, silent and helpless.

"I want to talk to you, Kate. Apparently tricking you and lying to you and tying you up are the only ways I can get you to listen to me." He paused, staring hard into her eyes. "It's important for you to understand that this is your fault. If you had not cast me off like an insignificant annoyance, you wouldn't be in this situation now. If you had just listened to me, if you had done what I said, our lives would be perfect." He paused for only a moment. "Now. You will sit right there, be a good girl. In time, I might even take that tape off your mouth if you promise no screaming. You will not like the result if you scream."

She nodded.

"I don't quite trust you, so the tape stays put until I've had my say."

He let go of her, but rather than move away, he righted the chair she had knocked over and then settled into it.

"You never wanted to share very much about yourself

with me, Kate, though you led me on, making me believe there was a future for us. No, don't frown like that, and stop giving me that confused expression. You came on to me—chased me, in fact. You know you did. It's all right there on that computer."

She stirred in her chair, and he went on alert. She forced herself to sit without moving as he launched into a diatribe about a bad childhood, tumultuous and ruined marriages, many disastrous relationships, children who refused to speak to him, and failed business ventures.

Kate listened to this account of his life. The more he talked, the more blame he placed on everyone else. She soon realized that everything except his unhappy childhood had come about because of poor choices he had made. Her naturally soft heart, however, did not ache for him, especially as she sat a virtual prisoner in his small computer room.

"Then you pursued me online," he said, tipping his head to one side as if measuring her worth, "and I thought my life had finally taken a turn in my favor."

All I did was ask you a question.

"Later, after you'd won my heart, I wanted to send you a token, a gift, and you refused, as if I were some kind of bum." His eyes narrowed, and she felt a frisson of unease, wondering if he had some punishment planned. "And then, before I could win you over again, you left me. No word of explanation. Just ... gone."

If he would remove the tape across her lips, she could explain why she chose to discharge his friendship from Friendlink.

"When I tried to reconnect with you, you ignored me." He let the statement hang between them for a moment as if he thought it would gain strength. Then he continued,

"What was I to do? I couldn't lose you, but Nick Scott had apparently lost Kate Stevens. I knew if I could connect as someone a woman like you would trust, I'd have a chance to win you. An old lady, a blind old man. But you weren't going to give me the time of day. I had to trick you, just so you'd listen to me."

He tilted his head a bit.

"Don't look at me like that." A small smile lifted one corner of his mouth. "You think I don't understand you. You think I'm being unfair. But it's you, Kate; you are the unfair one. The cruel one."

He rambled on, dipping into a story of his first wife and how she failed to understand him, support him, fill his needs.

Her phone rang and she stiffened.

He pulled the phone from his pocket and looked at it. "Well, well. Peter Matthews."

He looked up. "Are you expecting a call from your detective?"

She shook her head. Joe slid the phone back into his pocket.

"Then I believe we'll not talk to Detective Matthews right now." Joe patted his pocket and chuckled. "Good old Peter. I almost feel sorry for him. You know why? Because he wants you, but I have you."

Kate shuddered.

"You cold? You want a blanket?"

He left the room and came back a minute later with a soft blanket. He tucked it snugly around her.

Her phone signaled a text message. Joe took it from his pocket and looked at it.

"Well, looky there. Now you have a text from the great detective."

He stared down at the screen, then turned it so Kate could read it. *"R U OK?"*

Joe cocked his head to one side. "Well, are you? R U?" He grinned. "I love text messaging, don't you? Of course you do. It's like chatting, only shorter. I'll take care of this for you so Peter doesn't worry." He chuckled again. "Poor Peter."

Kate watched as he typed and sent the message. Joe slid the phone back into his pocket.

"Anyway, what was I saying? Oh, yeah, telling you about this one Christmas when my brother got the bicycle I wanted."

He finished the tale, his gaze staring at nothing, seeming to be lost in the memory. After a moment, he seemed to shake himself.

"I started to make us some fresh tea," he said, getting up. "This time, Kate, you will stay put while I'm out of the room, I guarantee it."

While he was gone, Kate struggled against her restraints. As much as she was able, she explored the back of her chair with her fingers, trying to find something to hold onto, something she could use as leverage as she struggled against her bindings. Then she felt something sharp and metallic. It was a screw, partially protruding from the old chair, its threads jagged and exposed.

Kate wriggled her wrists until the tape caught against the screw. She pressed and sawed, hearing the welcome sound of fibers being torn apart, bit by bit. It seemed that Joe might have underestimated her strength and ingenuity because it felt like he'd wrapped the tape only once around her wrists. Just as the tape began to loosen, he returned. "Fresh tea," he said as sweetly as if they were lovers. "I'll hold this for you and let you drink, but only if you promise not to scream."

She nodded.

"One scream, my love, and it's no more Mr. Nice Guy. Got that?"

Again she nodded.

"OK then. I hope this doesn't hurt." He put both cups down and tenderly peeled the tape from her lips. He picked up the cup, blew on it a moment, then held it to her lips. "Careful. It's hot."

She took a tiny sip, praying he hadn't put any kind of sedative in it.

"Good?" he asked.

She had to get him out of the room again. She thought fast, then forced herself to meet his eyes and give him a weak smile. "Joe, I'm not feeling so well. Could I trouble you for a piece of toast?"

He narrowed his eyes, and her heart skipped a beat. "Are you sick?"

Maybe if she played the role of a weak female, she'd catch him off guard. She nodded. "I have a queasy tummy. Tea and toast usually help."

He considered it for a few moments.

"OK. I'll fix you some toast. Maybe you need an antacid tablet?"

"Let's see if the tea and toast work first."

"All right." He set the cup aside, then taped her mouth again, saying, "Just in case you feel well enough to scream the minute I walk out of the room."

She sat stock still, counting to ten to give him time to be in the kitchen. She yanked her wrists as hard as possible and sawed against the screw threads. The last shred of tape ripped. The blanket slid from her and landed on the floor around her feet. She listened and heard Joe in the kitchen. As quickly as possible, she tore at the tape around her right ankle, tugging, yanking until she had freed it. She heard the toaster release the bread.

Frantically, she yanked on the tape around her left ankle. She heard Joe's returning footsteps just as she broke free. Less than three seconds after she'd tucked the blanket around herself, he came into the room bearing a small plate of toast.

"Here we are. A nice plate of toast and a warm cup of tea for my sweet girl."

She shuddered.

"Shivering, Kate? I hope you aren't getting ill." He laid a calloused palm against her forehead. "Maybe I should turn on the furnace."

She nodded eagerly.

"Listen, I'll come back and feed you this tea and toast, but first I'll go light the pilot on the heater. The furnace closet is just off the kitchen, so it won't take but a minute."

The moment he left the room, Kate looked around the room for anything she could use to stun him. She knew better than to try to escape without knocking him out, or at least slowing him down somehow. Trying to get to the bat where she'd dropped it at the front door was a long shot. She had to use whatever was nearby.

His chair. That straight, sturdy wooden chair that belonged at a dining table. She threw off the blanket, and hefted the chair. It was heavy, but she could handle it. She stood on the side of the door unseen from the hall. Her arms ached from holding the chair above her head, but she clenched her jaw and held on, waiting for him.

"There we go!" Joe called out. She heard him coming down the hall. "We'll have you a nice warm house in no time." He walked into the room, head down, dusting off his pants legs and sleeves. "I'll have to give that dusty space a good cleaning—"

He looked up and halted.

Before he could move, Kate brought the chair down on him as hard as she could. He crashed to the floor on all fours.

"Why you little—" he gasped.

He grabbed for her as she darted past him. She stumbled, but kept her balance and ran down the hall. She could hear him, roaring like an angry bull, coming after her.

She saw the bat, lying near the door. She had nearly reached it when the front door burst open.

Within the space of time it takes the heart to beat twice, the room filled with police officers. They had their weapons drawn, and all their guns were pointed at Joe. Voices filled the room as they surrounded the man, wrangling him to the floor.

Kate scrabbled backward toward the wall, out of the way, staring hard at the uniforms around her, her vision blurring, her ears buzzing and roaring as if a thousand volts of electricity coursed through her brain. She slid down the wall, her shaky knees giving way.

"Kate." The voice sounded faraway, and she could not find its source.

Bit by bit, her focus returned. The awful roar faded. The room emptied.

Well, not quite.

"Kate." Peter held out his hand and with great tenderness, helped her to stand.

Twenty-Two

Laughter and the good scents of the season filled the night's publishing party at Once Upon a Yarn in late November. Kate breathed deep, loving the homey scents of apple cider, cinnamon, and cloves.

She had been sharing the details of her recent ordeal for what seemed to be an eternity. Kate hated to be caught in the spotlight, but there was no escaping it this time.

Vivi turned to Peter. "How did you know you needed to rescue our fair damsel in distress?"

"It was the text Joe Vestal sent from Kate's cellphone," Peter explained. He pulled out his phone and summoned the message up, showing it to the group: "'2busy w/work 2nite. TTYL.' I knew Kate would never send a message like *that.*" He grinned at Kate. "I pay attention to what you like and don't like."

"I do wish Frieda would have come to the party," Kate said. "She had a hand in my rescue too. At least she accepted the banana bread I baked for her."

"I told you, she watches out for us," Vivi said. "It would have been better, of course, if she'd mentioned some of the suspicious goings-on at Joe's instead of doing her little tricks to ward him off. But calling the police about you going into his house when it wasn't safe was a great step for her. If they had taken her seriously, help would have arrived sooner."

"It's like the boy who cried, 'Wolf!'" Peter explained. "From what I understand, Frieda's calls to the police have always been about odd things, like the wind blowing too hard or an owl sitting in a tree during the day or a neighbor standing at a window too long. But when I received that text message from Kate's phone and called them, they knew something was wrong."

"Did you break any speed limits getting to her?" Adam asked, grinning.

"Yep." Peter sipped his cider and met her eyes over the brim of his cup.

Kate blushed and looked away.

"I think autumn is my favorite time of year," Adam said to the circle of friends near the faux fireplace. "A time of harvest and renewal."

"A time of gratitude," Paige added.

"Absolutely," Kate said. "I have so much to be thankful for this year. My move to Texas. Some wonderful new friends." She passed her gaze around to each of them. "A career doing something that I love. And I survived this latest mystery!"

Robin Gray, Kate's hardworking technical editor from Brighton & Craig, turned slightly to look at the evening gown Kate had so recently finished. It hung in all its elegant beauty on one of Paige's custom-made mannequins.

"I am in love with that gown, Kate," she said. "It's just the most beautiful thing I've ever seen."

They all turned to look at it, murmuring in agreement.

"Once I knew Joe was going to be locked away for a long, long time, I was able to start again and finish it," Kate said.

"You know I want one, right?" Vivi said, laughing.

"I know." Kate met her friend's eyes and smiled.

Vivi tipped her head to one side. "I can see you thinking. What is going on in that brain of yours, Kate Stevens?"

It was going to take some courage to say and do what she

was about to announce, but she knew it would be good for her. She wanted to continue to grow—as a friend, a designer, and a person. She drew in a deep breath and blew it out slowly, silently.

Kate looked at Paige. "About the fashion show?" She swallowed hard and gathered her courage. "I want to be the one who models the evening dress."

For a moment, silence greeted her as they all looked on in considerable surprise. She smiled.

"Hear, hear!" Alexus said, raising her glass. The rest of them—Vivi, Peter, Adam, Paige, and Robin—responded in kind.

Laughing with joy, Vivi added an exuberant "Way to go, Kate!"

Learn more about Annie's fiction books at

AnniesFiction.com

• Access your e-books

• Discover exciting new series

• Read sample chapters

• Watch video book trailers

• Share your feedback

We've designed the Annie's Fiction website especially for you!

Plus, manage your account online!

• Check your account status

• Make payments online

• Update your address

Visit us at AnniesFiction.com